INVASION

INVASION

ANIMUS™ BOOK TEN

JOSHUA ANDERLE

MICHAEL ANDERLE

LMBPN

DISRUPTIVE IMAGINATION®

Copyright © 2019 Joshua Anderle & Michael Anderle
Cover Art by Jake @ J Caleb Design
http://jcalebdesign.com / jcalebdesign@gmail.com
Cover copyright © LMBPN Publishing
A Michael Anderle Production

LMBPN Publishing
PMB 196, 2540 South Maryland Pkwy
Las Vegas, NV 89109

First US edition, December 2019
Version 1.01, December 2019
eBook ISBN: 978-1-64202-610-8
Print ISBN: 978-1-64202-611-5

Thanks to the JIT Readers

Diane L. Smith
Dave Hicks
John Ashmore
Kelly O'Donnell
Peter Manis
Jeff Eaton
Jeff Goode

If I've missed anyone, please let me know!

Editor
The Skyhunter Editing Team

DEDICATION

To Family, Friends and
Those Who Love
to Read.
May We All Enjoy Grace
to Live the Life We Are
Called.

CHAPTER ONE

Terra might have seemed an ironic name to those who didn't know the backstory to the first cloud city. These projects were created as an eccentric answer to humanity's expansion at the cost of the natural land. A group of scientists, developers, technicians, and others came together to create the self-sustaining platform. Architects and construction took over to create a magnificent city based on the capitals of culture and modern aesthetics such as London, Milan, Barcelona, Paris, and New York City.

In the center of this platform, in celebration of the upcoming peace agreements and new potential for worldwide cooperation, a massive tower was built, surrounded by a floating ring to symbolize unity. This structure would become the World Council Headquarters and what was first intended to be merely symbolic was now the actual domain of the new government that came to be. Terra would continue to act as a city of humanity rather than of only one nation.

On the eleventh floor of this building, Matek Asfour approached a data room with an escort of two guards. When he reached the door, he nodded at one of the cameras and held his badge up, which he then used to activate the locking terminal and open the door. What the cameras saw was him walk inside and to one of the servers while his bodyguards stood at attention at the entrance to the room. He was looking for several documents he would need for his upcoming discussion with delegates from Jordan, Iran, Sinai, and Egypt about the potential for a hyperloop crossing between the western part of the Middle East through the upper side of Africa. However, this was a false feed created by a trio of technicians and finished only the day before.

In fact, it was the opposite. Matek barely stepped farther than past the initial hallway and instead, immediately turned to the left and faced the wall while his two bodyguards moved deeper and began their actual mission. It was not to guard their councilmember—there was no need to guard an expendable golem—but to extract certain files and entire databases and leave viruses in their wake to be triggered at a later time.

Tory Harper, three floors above Matek and on the other side of the building, walked up to a guard post. Her intention was for a quick greeting and access to the military wing of the building. She slid her access card and ID into a small cylinder and waited for the green confirmation light. Instead, a red light flashed above the station and she frowned. "What is the meaning of this?" she demanded. "I was given approval two days ago. Check again."

The door to the military wing opened and a guard walked out and nodded to her. "My apologies, Councilwoman. Everything is indeed in order but we have new...complications."

"Explain," she instructed.

The guard looked around. Only a few other personnel and facility crew walked through the main hallway behind her. He nodded and leaned in. "The thing is, ma'am, that there have been some odd occurrences lately."

"Such as?" She allowed a trace of impatience to color her tone. "I understand wanting safety to be paramount in the Council, but I don't think we should be alarmed when someone misplaces their lunch or more than the average number of ID cards get lost."

He chuckled. "I wish it was that simple, ma'am, but it appears a few delegates have gone missing."

"Missing?" Tory stiffened. "Since when?"

"It hasn't been confirmed," he clarified. "but delegates Ronson and Chan haven't appeared in two days. Councilwoman Park has gone on vacation, but they haven't been able to get hold of her to discuss an upcoming agreement between Korea and Vietnam, and she has always been a stickler for being kept in the loop, even on vacation."

"I see, and you think something nefarious is going on?" she asked.

The guard shrugged as he straightened. "We can't be too careful at the cradle of humanity. We received orders this morning that no one can enter sections with a clearance of level two or higher without proper escort, even in what is probably the safest place in the building."

She sighed but nodded. "Very well, if you could take me to see the admiral, I would greatly appreciate it."

"At once, ma'am." The guard raised a hand and the red light turned green before he turned and the two walked into the military wing. They passed hurried men and women, some talking shop while others hastily finished reports to send to their higher-ups. Their route took them along the side of Command and she gazed at the numerous screens and consoles manned by dozens of people who coordinated possibly hundreds of missions at once.

"If you don't mind me asking," the guard said tentatively, "what are you here to discuss with the admiral? I hope you don't mind me prying, but when one of the Earth security councilmembers wants to see the admiral personally, well, that gets people talking—" He looked back but the councilwoman was gone. Startled, he turned his head first to the left, then the right and glimpsed a door close. Had she run in there? It was only a supplies room and he couldn't even imagine what she was doing.

The guard jogged over, opened the door, and walked in. "Ms Harper, what are you doing?" he asked as the door shut behind him. The glow strips activated automatically but when he tried to turn the main lights on, they wouldn't activate. Something clunked on the floor and he peered ahead and activated the light on his pistol. Tory had stooped to pick a gun up. "Hey-y!" He coughed and felt a little odd like he had swallowed a bug. "Councilwoman Harper, put that down imme—"

A sharp pain burned in his throat and he fell to his

knees. He coughed into his hand and looked down to see blood. His attempt to breathe gained him no air and he collapsed. He looked up and tried to focus on what he thought was a man clinging to the ceiling and dressed in a silver underlay with glowing gauntlets and a wide smile. The apparition waved at him and snapped his fingers. The guard's eyes twitched before they rolled into the back of his head and his brain erupted from within his skull.

Dario dropped from the ceiling and began to strip the guard of his armor. "We're on a short timetable as it is and they're catching on," he muttered and unlatched the chest plate as he motioned for Tory Harper's golem to fetch him a helmet. "Oh, well, it's much too late for them to do much of anything, even if they know what our plans are." He took the helmet the golem presented him with and put it on. "Thank you, dear. You can put the gun away. A different plan is in the works now that I am here."

She nodded and went to return the pistol. Dario considered the changes he'd decided on. It was actually mostly the same plan but instead of the golem killing the admiral and replacing him, the assassin would kill him while the golem began to change. That should have been the plan from the beginning as he would be able to take out the admiral and dispose of the body almost simultaneously.

He wondered how long the advantages they had created would last. The Park golem they had used to replace the general already showed signs of slowing mental function so was probably only viable for another couple of weeks. That would be enough to slow the council down and throw the military into disarray for a while, but the chain of command would correct that quickly enough. His team would have to rely on the terrorist and mercenary leaders they had negotiated with or replaced to keep the heat on while they acquired their other targets.

Dario donned the last of the guard's armor and removed the EI chip from the helmet. He stowed it in a compartment on the chest plate and slid his own in.

"Are you in, Giono?" he asked.

"Online, sir."

"*Bene.*" He beckoned the golem as he went to open the door. "Let us make sure that all the pieces are in place so the mission—and the fun—can begin."

CHAPTER TWO

"So the jockey gave me his pack and I was able to repair it while he and some of the riders held the droids at bay. He told me to put it on and escape while they pushed out of the building," Genos recounted and Kaiden listened in rapt attention.

"And you did? I told you those jetpacks were a nightmare," he stated.

"It was actually quite exhilarating," the Tsuna admitted and his eyes blinked rapidly with remembered excitement. "I'll admit, though, that if it wasn't for Viola's EI direction, I might have been a little out of my depth. But soaring through the skies, being able to find the right position at the right time, or even using quick-burst to leap back or to the side to avoid a shot or blow was a very exciting experience."

"I wish I could have been there with ya." The ace chuckled and took another sip of beer. "For most of the first half of the fight, I tried to find out where everything was. Then, when I got into the building, Chiyo and I took out that big bastard I told you about and—"

"Then the explosion happened?" Genos finished. "Yes, that was quite a shock but fortunately, I still had the pack when the fortress began to destroy itself. Escape was rather easy for me."

"It sounds like you took to it well," Kaiden mused as he checked his tablet. "You're an engineer so maybe for your last year you can take a workshop in jet packs?"

"I doubt there is something that specific, even in our vast curriculum," the alien responded but took a moment to think about it. "Perhaps I can enquire with the pilots and riggers and see if they have anything to offer."

"They would be your best bet, especially the riggers." He took another look at his tablet and frowned.

His companion noticed this and peered at the tablet as Kaiden leaned back and took another sip. "Are you waiting for a call from our friends? They still have some time before they have to meet up with us."

"Huh? Oh, not specifically, although I guess I'm looking out for them." He straightened and put his beer bottle to the side. "I'm waiting for a message from the big guys—Wolfson, Sasha, or Laurie. They found a ton of evidence from the files Chiyo was able to take and they are supposed to keep me in the loop on how everything is going."

"Has no progress been made?" Genos enquired and tapped his infuser nervously with irregular motions that seemed to try to form a pattern but failed.

"Actually, they had some progress almost right off the bat from what they told me," the ace revealed. "They had all the evidence and files compiled into a proper document and, thanks to some maneuvering on Sasha's part, were able to get it into the hands of some fairly powerful people on the council itself. The problem is that this is the council and even purely beneficial laws and agreements take a long-ass time to make it through. I can only imagine what the delay would be for evidence against an organization most people thought was merely a conspiracy."

"But our raid should have at least garnered some interest, yes?" Genos asked. "After all, the building exploded."

"Yeah, there was a huge amount of news coverage of that, which kind of complicated the matter when Wolfson revealed that he had a hand in it." He sighed. "He let slip that was where the info came from and that the base was fully armed and not simply a research outpost as it claimed in the licenses. Even so, more than a few people weren't happy that he took action instead of informing the government, police, or military. They said it broke several laws, to which Wolfson said that if they had done things the proper way, that building would still be standing while all the cops debated the best way to ask them nicely to go away. And, of course, he peppered his comment with several insults. Sasha had to step in and was able to keep Wolfson from getting detained, but he's basically under…island arrest, I guess? He's confined to the Academy for now."

"Oh, that is troubling," the Tsuna muttered and frowned at his purple cocktail.

"He's indifferent and says he spent most of his time at Nexus anyway and actually had time to catch up on work over the summer. I think he's starting to grow bored, though, since all he's had for practice are dummies and training droids." Kaiden chuckled. "For now, the evidence is being passed around. Sasha said that a few members and delegates of the council actually approached them of their own accord for more information and that some old military friends are interested. Even if the council doesn't take action for a while, they might get more done this way. Anyway, I wouldn't know as the last time I spoke to them was almost a month ago. Laurie finally messaged me yesterday and said they have more developments but disappeared when I responded."

"They are all busy, I'm sure. With the new year, even though we have the AO in our sights, we still have our main responsibilities," his friend pointed out. "Especially the...um, big guys."

"True enough," Kaiden agreed, but as he reached for his beer, his tablet dinged and his hand changed direction quickly to snatch it up. He looked at the screen with surprise.

"Have they responded?" Genos asked.

"No, it's Chiyo. I wonder what she—"

"Oi, Kaiden!" an Aussie voice called and the two looked up. Flynn, Amber, and Marlo strolled toward them.

"Greetings, friends," Genos announced and waved at the trio. "I began to think you didn't like us anymore."

"You've made enough of an impression for us to stick around," Amber teased.

"You three are the first to show," the Tsuna told them. "Do you know when the others will arrive?"

"They won't," Marlo replied and caught their attention. "At least not today. We actually came to get ya."

"For what?" Kaiden asked.

"Induction for fourth years has changed and it's happening tonight instead of tomorrow," Flynn answered.

"What? I didn't get any message about that."

"Did you turn notifications from the Academy off?" Amber asked.

He checked immediately and realized that he had when he'd tried to lessen the number of notifications he received in his anticipation for a reply from Laurie. "Dammit."

"I had...misplaced my tablet and left it at my abode," Genos admitted. "I intended to get a replacement once I checked in at the dorm."

"Well, it's a good thing we came to get ya." Marlo chuckled. "Grab some travel cups and let's move. We'll probably be late as it is."

Kaiden looked over to the bar and Julio caught his glance. "Hey, Julio, do you have some time?"

"What do you need?" he asked.

"A lift." The proprietor rolled his eyes but nodded and told a couple of the other bartenders to cover for him before he went to the back room.

"It looks like we'll be fine," the ace said and picked his drink up once more. "But to be safe, I'd better down this in one."

"Are you going to the ceremony buzzed?" Amber asked. "I'm sure that's smart."

"It's our last year," he replied, the bottle at his lips. "We can be a little irresponsible now, can't we?"

CHAPTER THREE

D*ear Kaiden,*
I wanted to leave a message to let you know that plans at the Academy have changed. They are holding our opening ceremony tonight. At first, I was concerned that this was due to our actions on some level, but Cyra assures me that timetables have been adjusted due to the influx of both new initiates and transfers this year. I only found out myself because I came in early to drop my gear and supplies off. As you aren't here yet, I assumed you had not received the memo. Please try to not be late as the others are already on their way.

We'll have to find the time to celebrate the new year later.
Chiyo

"Well, at least I wasn't the only one caught off-guard," Kaiden noted, turned the tablet off, and put it away. He leaned against the dropship wall and peered out the window for a moment at the forest they skimmed over.

"Okay, since we have some time…" Amber began and drew the ace's attention. "Didn't you say you would tell us what happened during your finals last year?"

"Huh? I already told you it was boring. It was only a retrieval mission for a device Laurie wanted that he couldn't be bothered to fetch himself," he replied and tried to avoid her gaze.

Flynn chuckled. "Come on, mate. Cameron said he saw you come back with Officer Wolfson and the commander, all of you with busted armor. That doesn't sound like a 'boring' retrieval mission."

"It was a very…intense retrieval mission?" Genos interjected and Kaiden shook his head.

Marlo folded his arms. "If you don't want to spill the details, I assume there must be a reason."

He nodded. "There would probably be some accomplice charges if you knew too much."

Flynn whistled and looked away, as did the demolisher. Amber laughed before she called to Julio in the cockpit. "You wouldn't happen to know anything, would you Julio?"

"No—or rather, I plead the fifth," he yelled in response.

She frowned and leaned against the wall. "You guys must have really been involved in something deep."

"Again, it's better for your own interests if you don't pry too much," Kaiden repeated.

"I concur," Genos added.

The medic rolled her eyes but smiled to show she wasn't upset by their evasion. The ship began to slow and Julio called, "We're reaching the Academy docks and have the all-clear. Get your stuff together and be ready to get your asses off my ship."

Marlo laughed as he stood and took his bag out of the compartment above him. "I'll give him points for speed and a smooth ride, but customer service could use some work."

"Did you buy a ticket?" Julio retorted and the demolisher snickered.

"I guess he heard you, Marlo," Flynn teased as he took an EI pad out.

His large friend nodded as he craned his neck. "I guess I'll hurry and get my ass off this ship."

The vessel circled the landing pad slowly and descended as the landing gear extended and the side door opened. Marlo made good on his word and leapt out before the ship even landed fully.

"Thanks for the ride, Julio!" Flynn yelled as he and Amber jumped out.

"Take care," Julio responded and waved to Kaiden and Genos as they prepared to exit. "Make sure to stop by soon."

"No worries. We gotta make up for not having drinks today," the ace promised. "Have a good one, Julio, and don't do anything too irresponsible."

He merely waved as his last two passengers dropped out. The door closed behind them as the ship ascended and banked sharply to return to Seattle.

Kaiden watched it for a moment before he looked at Chief. "Hey, send a ping to the others so we can get together. We're all supposed to be here by now, right?"

"It looks like someone beat ya to it," the EI announced.

"What?" He followed Genos to the stairs and when he looked down, his gaze settled on Flynn and the others greeting the rest of the group at the bottom.

"Flynn already alerted the others as we pulled in," Genos explained and slung his pack over his shoulder as he went down the stairs.

"Ah, well, you tried. Now get down there and remember, eye contact shows confidence."

The ace rolled his eyes and smiled as he slid down the stairway railing to greet his friends. He fist-bumped with Mack and Cameron and clapped Silas on the shoulder. "I'm glad we're all here. When's the ceremony?"

"In a couple of hours," Silas replied. "I'm surprised Durand was able to come up with something, considering he can't do his whole 'next level' speech now that we're still all technically masters due to tradition."

"It makes the fourth-year part mean a little more," Izzy agreed.

"I have heard that most fourth years are referred to as 'ascendants' by the others to distinguish them," Jaxon interjected.

"That actually sounds less cool," Cameron muttered. "I'm about to head to the dorms to get everything ready, but what say you guys to a little Animus training after the ceremony? We can get an early start."

"You probably only want to shoot something," Mack said mockingly. "Not that I'm opposed to the idea."

"I have to finish getting my workshop supplies tonight," Julius said. "And tomorrow, I have orientation in my exotech class."

"Are you looking into exotech?" Amber asked. "It seems a little late for that."

"Only to learn the basics. A fair amount of advancement has been made and in the future, they might be the new standard," Julius explained. "My skills as a biologist will still prove useful, but it's better to plan for the future, don't you think?"

"Agreed," Marlo declared. "That's why I started taking Rigger workshops last year. Working with mechs goes hand in hand with demolisher work."

"Don't worry, Cam." Kaiden placed an arm around the bounty hunter. "I'll join you. As much as I like the chancellor's little speeches, I would prefer something a little more...what's the word? Oh, exciting." He looked around the group. "Hey, have any of you seen Chiyo? I had a message that she was already here."

"It took me some time to make it over." The ace removed his arm from the bounty hunter as he turned. Chiyo smiled a greeting. "I was working on a project with Cyra. It's good to see you made it with enough time to spare, Kaiden."

"Fortunately, Julio is a barkeep with a pilot's license that should probably have been revoked by now," he explained with a chuckle. "But it's good for getting to your destination quickly. How have you been?"

"Quite well. I spent most of my time at Mirai and with my father..." Her voice trailed off but her smile did not waver. "It was nice seeing him again."

"I'm glad to hear it." Kaiden gave her a nod of approval before he looked around and over to the cafeteria. "I'd like to hear more about it, but I've had a couple of beers and flew on a ship so I'm...uh, rumbling a little. Do you know if the cafeteria is open?"

She nodded. "It is. Shall we go?"

"I could use a bite," Otto agreed.

"And I could use a couple of meals," Luke hollered. "Let's eat."

The group wandered over to the cafeteria as they

continued to talk and joke with one another. The first day of their last year was upon them. And, as they would soon learn, so were the machinations of the Arbiters.

CHAPTER FOUR

"If the mercenaries do not fall in line, you are to compel them to do so," General Nolan insisted and scowled at his two subordinates on the holoscreens. "They have been paid. If that is not to their liking, you have spare golems, I am sure. The attack will begin soon and we need the chaos their forces can sow for the mission to succeed. Do you understand?"

The two underlings nodded agreement, saluted the general, and turned their screens off. Nolan spun and left the office to walk out into the docking bay where the master carrier, all thirteen hundred feet of it, was going through final inspection and inventory. Dozens of troops were loading supplies and stock and a team picked a giant cylinder up and attached it to a loop of rings connected to the side of the ship.

Two guards supervised a group of mule droids as they brought the emitter on board, one personally designed by the organization's technicians based on the designs the EX-10 leader was able to recover. At least they were good for something. Almost everything was in place and for all his failings thus far, he was in his element now. He would make up for them.

"General!" a voice shouted happily from behind him. He turned to be greeted by Oliver Solos, who was dressed in a smart dark suit and a wide-brimmed hat and accompanied by at least four-dozen men.

"Mr. Solos," the general said with a nod and took another look at the man's entourage. "Who are they? Your personal escort?"

When Oliver came to a stop, he chuckled and clapped one of the men on their chest piece. "These, my good man, are some of the finest officers in my personal employ. I offer them to you as part of my gift to celebrate the big day."

"That's rather generous of you," he replied and studied the group with new interest. They were certainly well-armed and although he hadn't seen them in battle, Solos was not the kind of man to low-ball when it came to paying for such violent services. "Won't you need them for your personal defense? While I will secure our victory, there will still be a period of disorder as we establish ourselves. If you're not careful—"

"I've already made plans to be 'away' during all the action," Solos confessed and interrupted the warning. "I'll hitch a ride with Byson, Yadira, and Xiulan so there is no need to worry about me, my friend." He took a few steps forward onto the platform Nolan stood on and stared at the massive ship in front of him. "It is glorious. And it's amazing that we were able to build it in less than a year. Most projects of this scale take at least fifteen months."

Nolan gazed at the master carrier. The size of it dwarfed even most dreadnaughts that he had once commanded, and it would soon be filled to bursting with troops and droids to swarm the enemy. If the opposing forces had any competence, they would soon learn that they were outclassed and swing to their side. Merely thinking about it made him hope that his campaign would be quicker than he hoped. But, he reminded himself, hope was for morale, not strategy.

"You have Mr Pope and Ms Rosenfeld to thank for the quick build, as well as Mr Sasaki for paying the council into looking away from our factories," he explained.

"Ah, good old Juro. Did you hear he'll actually stay planet-side?" Oliver inquired with a mocking smile. "I bet he's hoping to be reinstated as the WC council leader once we're done with all this. A puppet position, of course, but a well taken care of puppet."

"We will need the order once the second phase begins," the general reasoned. "To bolster the forces and plan for the real threat."

"It really is a pity that it has come to this. We'll lose many potential soldiers for the next act. Ah, well, if we find what our leader is looking for at the Academy, we'll be able to make up for it easily. Speaking of which, here is the other part of my gift." He reached inside of his jacket, removed a small black box with an ouroboros symbol, and presented it to the general.

He took it and opened it to reveal a small, circular black device. "This is for their training system?"

The other man smiled. "Indeed, Dario retrieved it for me, and I had my technicians make the final touches. I had hoped to have it installed in one of my satellites so we could simply beam a signal into the system before we advanced, but I was unable to get my data and controls from my Normandy company holdings. The bounty hunter I sent to retrieve them failed—or simply disappeared."

That would have been a significant advantage, but once he had the Academy under his control, he would have access to their mainframe, an easy workaround. "It's ready to go, then?"

"It may need a few calibrations once installed. I'll send a few technicians to assist with that," Solos promised and his expression settled into a toothy smile. "I would recommend using the expendable hostages to test the first few batches."

Nolan closed the box, slipped it into his pocket, and turned away from the CEO. "That isn't something to take pleasure in, Solos. Those are sacrifices we must make like everything else."

"That's true enough," his companion said a little too loudly and tried hastily to restore the mood. "I'm merely delighted to see everything fall into place. After all, we've worked for almost a decade to bring this all together. And to see the Animus used for its proper purpose will be a treat."

With a click and a hiss, another large cylinder attached to the group of rings, the last one in that batch. The arms holding the rings swung back and brought the group within the ship before another set circled out to be filled. "They will be our guard when the time comes," the general stated cryptically. He turned and nodded at the other man once again. "I thank you for your gifts, Solos, but you'll have to excuse me. I must assist with the final preparations." He turned to look at the troops the CEO had brought with him. "You men report to Officer Brooks in section C. She will give you your orders and assign you to your units."

The troops saluted and walked away in formation. They were well-disciplined, at least. Solos watched them go with a satisfied grin. "I'll leave you to it then, General. I have a private vessel eagerly awaiting my patronage."

"I shall make sure you and the others are contacted when it is safe to return," he promised.

The man laughed and waved as he sauntered away. "At such a time, we will celebrate the victory of phase one."

Nolan watched him go and a feeling of disgust consumed him. Celebrate? He was one of the members who had contributed least to this moment. Still, when he felt the weight of the box in his pocket, he reminded himself that they all had their place in the plan.

Once phase one was a success, however, he doubted that Merrick would be in the mood to celebrate anything.

"Tell the captain to order his troops and battleship over to Samara," Merrick whispered into the speaker as he watched the admiral golem's meeting. "That mercenaries have made their way to Russia en masse so something is obviously underway and they need to be prepared."

He put the speaker down and smiled as the captain nodded and saluted when the golem's personality settings assumed control. Damyen was already in position, if his Ark Academy troops were even half as ready as he said they were, this would be an easy capture. It would add another battlecruiser to their arsenal and another group of recruits once they'd been properly trained.

The AO leader leaned back and frowned when the golem's heart rate line spiked briefly and erratically before it stabilized. The golems were reaching their limit and would give way soon but fortunately, it would be after they had launched their attack.

He glanced quickly at an activation switch propped up on a black mantle on his desk. Dario had confirmed that he was over eighty percent finished. Soon, the council as it was would change forever. Only a little more time was needed. He took a moment to let the certainty settle in and allowed himself a small smile. He would change the course of history with a few golems, some nanos, and a little camera tampering. One would think it would take more than that.

But they were not done, not yet. There would still be a war, a struggle they would have to face. And while he had no qualms about beginning and ending that war—they had prepared for it over a long period of time—he did hope that it would end quickly.

This was a war for the survival of humanity, after all.

CHAPTER FIVE

"From here on, I want you to climb to the tallest part of the mountain, to become something not only your underclassman can aspire to but your progenitors can find pride in and the world at large can see is among the best that humanity can offer," Durand announced to the auditorium. This elicited some cheers and claps from most of the crowd, some from excitement and others because they thought the speech was over. They would soon be proven wrong as he continued with how he looked forward to calling all those present victors soon. Kaiden was a little distracted when Cameron chuckled.

The bounty hunter leaned back and shared a look with his friend. "He does realize some of these guys will simply go into accounting, right?"

The ace shrugged, although an amused grin creased his face. "You have to admit, they will be kick-ass accountants, though."

"This has to be one of his longer speeches," Raul

muttered from Cameron's left. "Do you think he has it all memorized or is there a readout we don't see?"

"There can't be a readout. It would be too tempting for the hackers to mess with," Kaiden replied and nudged Chiyo to his right. "Ain't that right?"

Although it looked like she wanted to shush him, she sighed and conceded the point. "I can certainly think of at least a few of my fellow techs who would probably find it amusing."

"Personally, I think he's only saying what is on his mind," Genos commented. "Off the cuff, as you might say."

"He's probably done it enough that this is basically a greatest-hits of all his previous years," Cameron reasoned.

The ace tapped him softly on the chest. "Are you still up for some time in the Animus? It looks like this is almost at the end unless he gets a second wind."

"Oh, hell yeah," the bounty hunter agreed. "We'll round up those who wanna go once we hurry out of here."

Kaiden nodded as he focused his attention on Durand once again. The chancellor definitely seemed to be finishing up. "You shall prove yourselves masters of your class and emerge as victors who will set out into the world and stars to continue that legacy!" he declared in a booming shout. "Welcome to your last year, students. To victory!"

This time, there were cheers from all around the auditorium and a few eager students jumped up in excitement. He bowed and left the stage as the doors opened and students hurried out. The group of friends joined the exodus and emerged into the open air as the sun finally began to disappear and the purple and blue hues of twilight tinged the sky.

Otto, Julius, Izzy, and Indre all wished their friends well as they had to depart to finish their duties and prepare for the beginning of the year. The others headed to the Animus Center and the idea that this was their final year together seemed to occur to them at almost the same time, beginning with Flynn. "You know, this might be the last time we really work together for a long while."

"Yeah," Luke agreed and rubbed the back of his head. "Over the break, I started getting contract requests from security teams and the military. That totally made it real that I won't come back after this year."

"I guess I never thought about it too much," Cameron admitted. "I always knew where I would go. But I guess I'll be bummed not seeing you every day—even Kaiden and Raul."

"I'm so touched, really." Raul chuckled, although it didn't last as the general mood of the group had lost its jovial tone.

"I suppose we'll have to make sure we stay in contact through the network," Chiyo suggested and looked at Jaxon and Genos. "But will that be possible for you two? You'll head back to Abisalo once you've graduated, correct?"

"That is the current plan." Jaxon nodded. "Although there are rumors that a few Tsuna graduates will actually be contracted here on Earth in select companies to improve relations. If it goes through, it will be on a volunteer basis. It is a big decision as those Tsuna who remain won't have many opportunities to return home for an extended period of time until their contract is up."

"I may even need to have further schooling for a time," Genos admitted. "I've worked equally with human and Tsuna machines in repairs, modding, and construction. But when I was home over the break, I could see that there were already vast improvements to much of our technology and weaponry. I need to get reacquainted."

"To answer your question, though, Chiyo, the connection between Earth and Abisalo has been vastly improved," the Tsuna ace added.

"Oh yes." The mechanist nodded eagerly. "There may be some latency issues and the like, but you should have no problems contacting us should we return. Even then, I've received your messages fine, as you know."

"I'm glad." She smiled. "Especially with how fast you reply. Even with the delay, you're technically faster than Kaiden is most of the time."

"I'm working most of the time!" Kaiden retorted. "How are we almost three years in and I'm still the whipping boy?"

"You probably wanna make sure that whoever you work with next doesn't get that impression so early on," Marlo joked.

"Speaking of which, what will you do, Kai?" Flynn asked. "I remember you said you want to start your own merc company. Will you be able to do that by graduation?"

"I'm getting all the licenses and stuff approved but it took more time and creds than I was quoted," he muttered. "I need to create channels so people can reach me and get a ship for planet travel and outfit it for space travel as well.

Even with my current rank, I'll probably start out low on the totem pole. But since I'll be mission-focused instead of only a hired gun, I should advance fairly quickly to getting decent work in about a year."

"Do you have any idea where you'll find a crew?" Amber asked.

"I doubt you'll simply call at the merc ports and bars and find who'll work at the cheapest rate," Silas reasoned.

"Yeah, no," he said flatly. "Nexus grad or not, you have to have a good crew if you don't want your merc company to implode, even I know that and at best, I could be called 'savvy' rather than smart when it comes to business matters."

"So do you have any particular people in mind?" Amber inquired.

"A few," he admitted and although he didn't turn his head, his gaze darted briefly to Chiyo. "But whether I get them or not will be up to them when the time comes. I have to make sure everything else is in order before that can happen."

They reached the center and Luke approached the door, but it didn't slide open for him as it usually did. He frowned slightly and tugged on the handle but it didn't budge. "Uh...it doesn't look like its open."

"I guess things are a little disorganized," Flynn commented. "Most of the lights in the main lobby are off too."

Chiyo raised her arm and a holoscreen appeared over her gauntlet. "Let me give Akello a call."

It took only a couple of rings before the head monitor answered but she seemed distracted. "Put that over there, and Viko, double-check to make sure that halls thirteen through sixteen have enough power." She turned to face the screen. "Hiya, Chiyo—oh, and all you guys."

"Hi, Akello." They greeted her almost in unison as they peered over the infiltrator's shoulders at the screen.

"What can I do for you?"

Kaiden raised his hand. "If you could open the doors that would be nice."

Chiyo rolled her eyes. "We were hoping to have some early Animus training, but the doors are locked and it looks like the lobby is dark. I take it you are still preparing the center?"

The woman nodded and glanced behind her at a different monitor. "Yeah, sorry about that. We usually have it on by now, but Laurie and his team ran a whole...whatever it was. While it upgraded the system and even let us power more pods in here, we're still trying to find out the exact number that we can have running at once. It looks like we've resolved it for the most part but it's caused some delays."

"I guess that means we won't be able to get in tonight, huh?" Luke asked.

Akello pursed her lips as she considered it before she snapped her fingers. "Actually, we do need to do a test run. You guys could probably put the Animus through its paces better than a group of us. We still need a little time but if you could show up promptly at five in the morning, I'll make sure you get in."

"Five in the morning?" Raul almost gasped. "I need my beauty sleep."

"Pray really hard that you don't end up in the military, Raul." Mack chuckled and clapped him on the back.

"I'm still game. I have nothing else to do tonight so I'll be ready," Cameron confirmed.

"I was free tonight but I have a workout group I gym with in the morning tomorrow," Silas said regretfully. "I don't wanna skip out on the first day."

"I'm part of that group too," Luke added.

"Okay, who's still in?" Kaiden asked and Cameron, Jaxon, Genos, Flynn, Chiyo, Amber, and Marlo raised their hands. "Okay, with me that makes eight. That's enough for a team skirmish or something."

"Will that do, Akello?" Chiyo asked. The ace's eyes lit up as Chief showed him a new message.

The head monitor nodded. "That works for me but be sure to be on time. We need to have this ready by eight and the test run is the last step."

"We'll be here," the infiltrator promised.

Kaiden gave her a wave. "Have her purring for us!" he stated as he tapped Chiyo on the shoulder and gestured for her to follow him once she hung up.

Akello said goodbye and signed out. The group began to disperse to their dorms for the evening, wished each other well, and promised to meet the next day as Kaiden and Chiyo headed toward the R&D department.

Tomorrow promised to be busy indeed.

CHAPTER SIX

Laurie, Sasha, and Wolfson turned and greeted Kaiden and Chiyo as they entered Laurie's office. She returned the friendly smiles, as did the ace in a somewhat distracted way as he was more interested in looking at a small black band on Wolfson's wrist.

"The head of security is being monitored?" he asked with a smirk. "For our security or his?"

The large man scowled but before he could retort, Sasha stepped in. "It's placatory, Kaiden. And while I usually don't mind you and Wolfson and your little quarrels, you should know that it could potentially have been you wearing that band."

"Oh, I'm aware of that." He leaned against the edge of one of the couches as Chiyo sat. "Although I doubt I would have been let off with something as simple as a security band."

"You'd spend your last year in a cell while the trial was delayed by new paperwork almost every day," Wolfson snarked. "Gits. They are happy to take the evidence but still have to pretend that there were legal means to get it."

Chiyo straightened. "I know that the data has been delivered, but is it finally getting looked at in an official capacity?"

"Yes…and no," Laurie admitted. The ace shook his head.

"I replied to your message but you never responded, Laurie," he said and tapped his chest. "Now that I'm here, do you finally want to explain what's going on?"

Laurie pushed his seat back and stood. "It wasn't that I was trying to keep you in the dark. It's that we don't exactly know where all the pieces are at the moment."

Wolfson sighed and leaned against the desk. "We have supporters on the inside, mostly old contacts of mine or Sasha's who have found themselves nice positions in the WC, as well as a few delegates who have investigated suspicious happenings in the council on their own."

Chiyo tilted her head. "If anything illicit was happening in the council, wouldn't you have been notified? It sounds like this would have been a smoother process."

"Suspicious happenings, Master Kana, not illicit," the commander clarified. "Although one will eventually bleed into the other once no answers are found."

"What kind of suspicious?" Kaiden enquired. "Anything like what happened in the Animus?"

"From what we have been told, for the last couple of years, files have gone missing or odd discrepancies have occurred in scheduling and the like," Laurie explained.

"Things that would make even the most apathetic guard take notice," Wolfson continued and shook his head. "Not that there are any in the WC."

"They have looked into these issues internally but have come up with nothing to say that it wasn't anything more than a bad readout or some other small issue that could be attributed to faulty procedure. Although this created enough concern that a task force was created to comb through the system and all hard drives in search of the 'internal issue,' it only brought up more questions."

"The data you brought in that we sent out got the task force all riled up, as they found some of the missing files along with others that were obviously copied from their stores," the security head stated and threw his hands up in irritation. "That should have made any of the remaining missing pieces click together and it did for some. The council, however, doesn't like to think that anything on the scale of an all-out attack could be successful without them already knowing about it. They've spent too long with their only real problems being politics and the occasional terrorist group causing chaos before being eradicated or forced back into hiding by the military."

The former sergeant huffed and glared at the band on his wrist. "Instead of thanking us for giving them a lead and destroying a potential enemy stronghold, they took us to task for attacking it at all and went on about the loss of life and the damage to the environment from the explosion. I expected all that, personally, but the fact that they act like there's nothing to be concerned about from what we found and that we are the real problems still stirs my blood."

Kaiden gritted his teeth and looked away. "I know it's the stereotype that politicians look out more for their personal interests than the problems right in front of them, but if this is really the furthest we've progressed because of their incompetence, we're either screwed or they've already been taken over by the AO."

"That is a possibility," Sasha replied and Chiyo and Kaiden turned to him with wide eyes. "You didn't already believe that could be the reason?" he questioned. "Our investigation started under the assumption that WC members were a part of the AO. If that is still true, they could have already grown their web for years—far longer than we've searched for them."

"Before you have a heart attack," Laurie interjected and walked around the desk and over to Kaiden. "Those connections I told you about have already started their own investigations. In fact, a few have told me they have identified facilities similar to the original one you found in Germany."

"The underground base?" the ace asked.

The professor nodded. "These are smaller facilities, but if an official team or taskforce actually finds one themselves, that would force any doubters to take the situation seriously."

"Indeed," Sasha nodded. "That's the plan. Several teams are being prepared to raid these under direct orders of affiliates and delegates. Once the bases are shut down, they will make an announcement to the council who will have to announce it to the public."

"Meaning the organization will no longer be able to simply hide anymore. Everyone will be looking for them," Chiyo suggested.

"They'll still be a threat," Wolfson added. "But with the

full force of the WC ranged against them, they won't be able to put up a fight for too long."

Kaiden smiled. "I guess I shouldn't be too happy until we hear the results of the raids, but I have to admit I'm disappointed that I won't be there to see those shady bastards finally toppled."

"It was you who brought them to light in the first place, Kaiden," Sasha stated. "Remember that."

"And if you work hard enough, you might graduate in time to find yourself a team and see if you can get in on the action," Wolfson suggested and stroked his beard thoughtfully. "Although that would require you to join the military, which is still a good choice."

The ace held his hand up to stop him. "I have my own plans, although I'm sure there'll be fallout after the organization is crushed. Maybe I can get some gigs and closure that way."

"How long until the attacks on the facilities?" Chiyo asked.

Laurie sighed. "There have been some delays, unfortunately. They should actually have happened this week but the general in command has shipped troops out to dozens of different locations. It apparently has something to do with potential terrorist cells being discovered."

"Those in charge of the raids have had to tighten and focus their efforts, but they should begin their missions within the next few weeks," Sasha confirmed.

"A few weeks, huh?" Kaiden muttered and looked at Chief. "At least the noose is tightening, right?"

"I guess so," the EI responded. "If the truth be told, the waiting might be the hardest part."

Merrick watched and listened in on the conversation in Laurie's office via the tiny bug placed by one of the board members they'd subverted. At the end of it, he had to give the Nexus staff credit. With only a handful of them, they had managed to cause such large problems for him that a significant amount of course correction had been necessary during the last year.

Although in the end, it simply required a change of plans and had put the Academy on the top of his priority list. It had always been there, but he had hoped to acquire Nexus through subterfuge and guile. It would mean fewer lives lost that way. Now? He would take it by force and he would once again be the head of the Academy, although for very different reasons.

"Sir?" A screen appeared on his left and he glanced at Jiro and Karimi as they came into focus. "The cells are in position. Once the invasion begins, we'll keep the military forces occupied here in Asia."

"Understood. We shall hopefully have the council building under our control in only a few days." Merrick's focus returned to the screen that displayed Laurie's office. "And from there, we can prepare for the real threat."

CHAPTER SEVEN

The sun had barely begun to peek out above the hills and manmade structures that surrounded Nexus island. The light glinted faintly off the lake water and the artificial lighting had slowly begun to dim. Groups of students wandered the plaza, old friends meeting up or newbies trying to still find the paths that led to their workshops.

Cameron yawned and stretched, and his arms almost knocked against Kaiden and Flynn as the trio walked out of the cafeteria with plastic mugs of coffee. They made their way over to the rest of their group and passed out the various orders of coffee and juices before they once again proceeded to the Animus Center.

"She's ready for us, right?" the bounty hunter asked between what was basically chugs of caffeine. "Akello, I mean. We won't have to loiter around the entrance to the AC, will we?"

"She's there," Chiyo confirmed. "She's on my network and I've already sent a message that we're on the way."

"Do you have her position? She only gave me her commlink code," Kaiden muttered.

"You two seem to have a…strained relationship," Jaxon said and unlocked the mouthpiece of his infuser to sip the juice Flynn had gotten for him.

"What? Naw, she digs me," the ace protested.

"In spurts, certainly." Chiyo giggled and stowed her tablet in the messenger bag across her chest. "She said the doors are unlocked and she'll meet us in hall 001."

"Good, no stairs," Marlo noted and rolled his shoulders. "I have to remember to stretch before we get into the pods."

"I stretched almost as soon as I got out of bed," Amber stated. "I had to get the blood going, especially this early."

"Might I ask what training we will participate in?" Genos asked. "Or will it be a war game?"

"I'm up for some elimination," Cameron suggested. "Free for all or teams. We could make teams of four or go in pairs."

"I would suspect that is up to the head monitor," Jaxon reminded them. "Although if we do have a vote, I would like a team competition."

"We are christening the Animus for the beginning of the year," Kaiden said. "I think it would be proper that we start with some elims."

"Proper?" Amber asked and looked at him with a grin. "Is Flynn rubbing off on you after all this time?"

"Aussie, not British," Flynn reminded her and took a sip before he elbowed her. "And what are you poking fun at me for? You're Aussie too but with no accent."

"I moved around too much for it to stick, really," she admitted.

"If we do teams, how will we decide on who goes into which one?" Marlo asked.

Kaiden looked around. "I guess we can either divide into our normal teams and have Cam and Jax flip a coin, or we can have one of our EIs randomize it."

"I'll make sure your team is 'interesting,'" Chief promised, although the hint of mischievous implication in it was not well hidden. Given that all his options were his friends and all of them well experienced by now, he wasn't sure how the EI would mess with him, but he also knew Chief was crafty.

"If we do the latter, I won't volunteer Chief," he announced and the EI's eye shrunk and his avatar turned red as a few members of the group chuckled.

"Well, now I want to see how that would turn out." Flynn chuckled as they reached the entrance to the AC. Most of them tossed their disposable cups into the trash before they went in. The building was illuminated only by glow strips and a few lights above.

"It doesn't look like it's completely online yet," Amber said before they all heard a large hum and the main lights came on. "Oh, well, never mind then."

"Hall 001 is open," Marlo called and smiled as he looked inside. "And someone's already here."

The group entered and looked at Akello, who waited at the main console. She turned and waved them over with a warm greeting. "Morning, guys. Are you ready to be the first students in the Animus for the year?"

"You bet!" Kaiden nodded and glanced at the pods

closest to the console as they activated and the doors slid open. "What do you have for us?"

"I thought I'd leave that up to you guys," she replied and brought up the mode and map options. "Everything is ready and we even have some new maps. What are you looking for?"

The group looked at each other and most nodded as they had already agreed to their preference on their way in. "We'll go with team elimination," Jaxon stated. "As for the map, perhaps we should try one of the new ones?"

"It sounds like fun!" Amber agreed. "What are the teams?"

"Honestly, I simply want to get started already," Kaiden admitted. "Let's go with Flynn's group and mine. We'll take Jax as our fourth member."

"Pulling rank there?" the marksman questioned sarcastically and motioned Cameron over, and the four of them went to the pods on the left side of the console.

"If he whines too much, we can swap after the first match," the ace retorted and glanced at Akello. "Speaking of which, is the best of five all right?"

She nodded as she scanned the map list. "Sure, but let's try to make good time on this, okay? I have loadout training with the first group of initiates in a few hours."

"It'll be fine, Akello," Flynn promised as he entered his pod and grinned at Kaiden as the door closed. "It won't take us too long to kick their asses."

The ace rolled his eyes as the door to his pod began to close. "You'll come out of that pod sobbing," he promised and darkness enveloped him momentarily before the pod lights activated. He leaned back and closed his eyes. He had become so used to the sensation of connecting to the Animus and it seemed incredible to think this would be his last year using it.

Wolfson stood at the edges of the docks and let the early light of the sun warm him. He received a call on his comm. "Talk to me," he ordered.

"Sir, we seem to have odd readings from two of the relays in the hills," one of his officers responded. "Some of the cameras seem to be malfunctioning too."

"Also in the hills?" he asked as he turned to look in the direction of the town across the bridge. "That's the police's jurisdiction. We're only notified if it's our students causing problems."

"They are requesting help with maintenance, sir," the officer explained. "They said they had their techs look at them but they can't find anything. Their best guess is that it might be something with the software."

"That's Laurie's boys." Wolfson grunted, took his tablet out, and looked at his messages. There was nothing from the professor, which was odd. Laurie always took pride in his designs, no matter how insignificant. If something was wrong with any of them, he would be the first to know and send a message out, even if it was only a few words, that he would handle it.

"I can't make it over myself," he stated, put the tablet away, and hurried to the R&D building. "But I'll let Laurie know. If he hasn't received a message about it already, something must be wrong with the connection. He would get an alarm if something was corrupted."

"Understood, sir. I'll let them know," the officer stated and signed off. As Wolfson made his way to Laurie, he glanced at the sky. His brow furrowed when he noticed, far off into the distance, something strange about the clouds—or, rather, one massive cloud that stretched across the horizon. Perhaps he was still shaking sleep off, but an ominous feeling settled over him.

Unconsciously, he began to pick up the pace.

CHAPTER EIGHT

"*Team elimination, best of five rounds. Map: District 99.*"

The artificial voice rattled off the details as Kaiden fell through a neon-lit tube. The lights gradually fell away until he could see through the clear lining. Below him sprawled an empty city of modern design with neon lights and swirling colors gliding through the air. It made a damn pretty sight, he had to admit. He looked to his left to locate the other members of his team. Genos, Chiyo, and Jaxon fell through tubes like his, all now dressed in their loadout gear. He looked across the map at four specks in the distance—Flynn's team—and he could swear he could make out Cameron flipping him off in the distance. It would be fun to get him back.

The speed of his fall began to slow as the artificial gravity kicked in. He drew Sire as the tip of his left foot made contact with the landing pad below. When his teammates alighted, they also drew their weapons and huddled together.

"Hey, Jax." Kaiden beckoned and shouldered his rifle. "I'll lead this round and you take the next?"

The Tsuna ace nodded. "Very well. Orders?"

"Teams of two," he stated and held two fingers up for emphasis. "You and Genos. I'm with Chi. They might stay in a group but both Flynn and Cameron like the whole lone wolf approach. We might catch them alone."

"In that case, Amber will definitely stick with Marlo," Chiyo pointed out. "A battle-medic and heavy is a dangerous combination."

"Only as long as her gadgets are working," Genos suggested and held out a nano grenade. "It's a simple enough fix."

"She'll have some kind of purge, though. And even if we take her out, Marlo will be a handful. If there's anyone more gleefully destructive than me it's a demolitionist," Kaiden reasoned. "Keep a lookout and Chief?"

"Do you have something for me?" the EI asked and materialized in the air.

The ace gave him a thumbs-up. "Take a look around but be careful, though. I'm sure Cameron has a drone looking for us."

"On it." The EI nodded and floated upward. The holographic ambient lights actually allowed the orb to blend in with the sky and hide a little better. Kaiden watched him fly off, then checked the top left of his HUD to confirm that their vision was still connected. He nodded to Jaxon and Genos who returned the gesture before both leapt off the pad, down to the ground, and hurried away to the left side of the map.

Kaiden watched them go for a moment, then noticed a door on the other side. "Do you wanna take a stroll or—" Before he could finish, he looked back and Chiyo dove off the pad herself, flipped in the air, and landed several stories below.

She straightened and looked at him. "Are you coming?" she asked over the comms. He simply smiled under his mask before he stepped casually off the edge and fell to the ground beside her.

"So, who are you looking to bring into your company?" Chiyo asked as Kaiden peered around a corner. His gaze darted from his visor to Chief's viewing feed.

"Company?" he asked, momentarily distracted. "Oh, the merc company?"

"Right. You said you had some people in mind," she prodded.

He gestured for her to move closer as they crept through the alley. "I do but don't know if it's even possible to get them, really. All but one of them are contracted."

She tilted her head. "And the one who isn't is…"

The ace glanced over his shoulder for a moment. "You," he stated and returned his focus to the way ahead when they left the alley. They stood in the middle of a brightly lit street where glowing signs advertised fake restaurants and hotels above them.

"I finally got you to say it." She chuckled, looked at the roads, and pointed to the one in the center.

Kaiden nodded as they continued to advance. "I guess I didn't want to seem like I simply assumed you wanted to throw your lot in with me," he admitted. "You're as free as I am now and have a ton of options. Chief still reminds me that even though we're both 'special cases,' you were actually invited and I was only recruited."

"And I told you I took the invitation to find my own path," she replied. "You don't think it's possible that path could be with you?"

"It could be, although I don't know many people who would take the path over the cliff over the golden path." He chuckled, caught movement in his peripheral vision, and took aim. Almost immediately, he lowered his rifle when he realized it was simply an animatronic advertisement. "That's annoying."

"It might be a path that leads to a cliff, but there could be exciting things over the edge," she countered coyly.

Kaiden chuckled. "Isn't that romantic."

Chiyo passed him and made her way into another alley. "It could be that too."

He stopped for a moment and smiled but his thought was interrupted by Chief. *"We have a problem, partner."*

"Did you find them?" His gaze darted to the feed.

"No, but I wanted to let you know the sky is falling."

His feed revealed the truth of this, although there seemed to be no explanation for it. He pressed a switch on the side of his helmet to sharpen his view of the sky as tendrils of white spread above and the buildings around them began to fade.

The infiltrator lowered her weapon and frowned at the

disappearing buildings before she looked at him with real concern. "The Animus is shutting down." She opened a holoscreen. "Akello, what's going on?"

"All of you need to get out," the woman ordered, a worried tone in her voice. "Now!"

"Do you think we should have gone to the AC with Cameron and the others?" Izzy asked as she set her tray down. "I thought I would sleep in, but I was so excited for the first day that I ended up waking up before my alarm even went off."

"I didn't sleep much either," Otto confessed and gestured to Julius. "Although I was working on a new program, something to help Julius make new chems and salves on the fly. All he would have to do is link up his—"

Indre almost dropped her tablet when it began to flash red. "What? What did I do?" She recoiled as **Warning** flashed over the screen. The others checked their tablets and confirmed that all their alarms had been activated as well.

"Is this a drill?" Izzy looked confused.

"No, they wouldn't do that on the first day," Julius reasoned. "The initiates wouldn't know the procedure."

"Then this is real?" Otto placed his tablet down. The dozens of other students in the cafeteria area looked at one another in consternation and some rushed outside. "What's going on?"

"Get out of the way!" Luke shouted as he, Silas, Raul, and Mack pushed their way out of the soldiers' dorm. "Come on, people. Move!"

The entrance hall was bottle-necked as all the remaining students in the dorm attempted to rush out at the same time. Many weren't even properly dressed and some even wore nothing but a towel as the dorm alarm had blared in the middle of their morning shower.

Luke and Mack were able to force a small opening for them to push through and finally made it out the doors. A large group of students stared into the sky, wide-eyed. The friends looked up as well and their heart rates increased and breath hitched when they saw something massive break through the clouds.

Wolfson barged into Laurie's office. The alarms in the building had activated almost as soon as he had stepped in and he now yelled orders into his comm while he searched for the professor.

"I want all security bots activated and on patrol. Send all armored guards to the plaza and get everyone suited up. I want drones in the sky and flyers warming up." He signed off when he saw Laurie behind his desk, staring at his monitor screen in shock, his face pale and lips pursed.

"Laurie! What the hell is going on?" he demanded.

The professor snapped out of his frozen shock and pressed a button on his board. A massive holoscreen appeared behind him to display the feed of a camera on the edges of the island. The security officer stopped in his tracks when a titanic ship broke through the clouds and descended toward the island. They watched in disbelief as several cannons took aim at the Academy, activated, and fired.

CHAPTER NINE

"It is now eleven o'clock in the evening and only three world council delegates arrived for today's debate out of a total of ten. There has been no response to queries as to the other delegates whereabouts and it would appear the debate will be canceled for the evening."

Anne Myers, one of numerous secretaries in the world council building, tried to tune out the news playing on the monitors above while she made her way over to the general to decide on an answer to the news story. At least four delegates were supposed to represent the military and not a single one had done so. If she had to personally remind the military leader of how important these discussions were for both discourse and public perception, she would, and not happily either.

However, what she was greeted with once she barged into his office immediately changed her anger to confusion and finally, fear. When the door slid open, a smell of mold and curdled milk almost made her gag. She staggered back and blocked her nose when she noticed a white liquid dripping from the general's chair. His hat and clothes slid off, coated by the mysterious liquid as well a mixture of blood, hair, and yellow pus.

Her eyes widened and she spun to race out to the lobby and find the nearest guard. Fortunately for her, one was coming up the hall as she began her sprint. She almost fell over herself as she slid to a stop and pointed behind her. "The general—something happened...he disintegrated..." She babbled in her effort to formulate a coherent sentence and continued to point frantically behind her as she looked at the guard. To her horror, small pockets formed on his cheeks.

"It was time," he said in a monotone, and the same rancid smell from the general's office flowed out of his mouth as he spoke. Anne recoiled from the guard, who simply raised his rifle and fired at her.

"Ma'am, I have another call!" one of the security officers yelled. "Another lobbyist has turned to mush in the middle of the conference hall."

The co-chief of security bit her lip. This latest report made almost twenty calls, all identical. Delegates, lobbyists, and military personnel all suddenly dissolved into liquid matter. No one recalled them yelling in pain or surprise and in fact, in a couple of cases, it was reported that limbs had fallen immediately before their deaths. What the hell was going on?

"Could this be some kind of nano attack?" she asked no one in particular, but she did get a response from above.

"I can promise that it wasn't me." She looked at a man who smiled at her from where he held himself on the ceiling with adhesive grips, his expression amused. Instinctively, she reached for her gun, but with a snap of his fingers, her head erupted. The other officers tried to draw their weapons quickly, but with another snap, more than a dozen men and women lost their lives in small but bright flashes.

Dario dropped from the ceiling and retrieved two tablets as he walked over to one of the consoles. He plugged one of these in and let it boot up while he scrolled through the other.

"We really did cut it close," he mused quietly when he saw that there were only six timers remaining. Each counted down to the approximate deadline for the golems. "Fortunately, the replacements are made of more durable material." He changed screens and pressed a green activation button before he set that device aside when the other finished booting up and accessed the system.

In the hangar bay of the council building, several guards jogged over to the group of messenger ships in the corner of the east wing when they heard loud bangs from within.

"Is anyone on board?" the leader asked and cautiously approached the rear entrance of one of the ships, his weapon ready.

"No, sir," an officer answered. "These came in this morning, all automated."

"And they weren't checked? What's in—" His question

cut off abruptly when the door hurtled off the back of the ship and into him and a large group of white-and-silver Arbiter droids surged from the vessel. The guards tried to fire but were incinerated by the mechanicals' plasma cannons. Other ships began to fall apart and revealed more of the invaders that immediately began to scatter. Some intercepted incoming guards while others forced their way out of the hangar and made their way deeper into the building.

***

Dario watched the monitors as the droids began their attack and noted that there were probably a little over a hundred all in all. They should be enough to maintain the chaos, but the guards would regroup sooner or later and they still had the numbers advantage. He picked the connected tablet up and smiled as he pressed a button and initiated the lockdown procedure. That should cause a few delays.

Alarms began to blare and the shields activated throughout the building. The assassin smiled as he pressed a few more keys and began the more important part— uploading the virus. Once it had settled in and assumed control, he would be able to send it to any other machine or ship connected to the WC. That, in his opinion, would make the fight a little fairer.

He took out an EI pad and instructed his device to contact Merrick. In short order, the AO leader appeared in hologram form. "What do you have to report, Dario?"

"Phase one is well underway now," he stated as he

checked the tablet's progress. "I'm sure Jensen did good work on this virus, but it looks like it will take some time before it loads."

"Are you worried that you may be caught and stopped before the upload can finish?" Merrick questioned.

"Caught? Perhaps, but I certainly won't be stopped," he promised. "Although I will say I do hope that Nolan had the gift prepared before his departure. I'm not certain how long our current forces will last."

"I would think you would relish the chance to have your fill of violence." His boss chuckled and he simply smiled in return and shrugged nonchalantly. "Don't worry, my friend. The destroyer is on the way."

"Splendid. When will it be here?"

"According to the captain's terminal, ETA is in an hour."

"Captain's terminal? Are you the captain?" Dario asked, amused as he leaned casually against his console. "Did you decide to join the fun yourself?"

"It's where I am needed most," Merrick stated, a look of determination on his face. "I trust Nolan to take care of Nexus and for everyone else to fulfill their parts. But making sure to topple the council's systems and bring them under our control is top priority. Everything else is to ensure we have the best opportunity to do so."

"Understood." The assassin looked up when someone pounded on the plated door and guards called frantically for assistance. "I have to go for now." He activated his nanos and walked to let in the new guests. "I'll see you soon, *capo*."

CHAPTER TEN

The protective dome over the island had somehow been disabled and Nexus students sprinted out of the way of the falling pods. Some ran into buildings while others tried to pull or push others in their path who were too shocked to move. Security bots flooded the plaza seconds before loud hissing issued from each of the grounded pods. Four sections on each disengaged and Arbiter droids emerged. Their eyes flickered to life as they scanned the students around them.

There seemed to be a dozen droids per pod, and more and more landed on the island. Even those that plunged into the lake didn't falter and some students hurried away from the edges of the island as blue lights could be seen in the water only a few seconds after the pods crashed.

The security bots ordered the students to get back. Many of them helped to escort them to safer areas while others prepared to engage, but they were not as well armed as their adversaries. Most were equipped with shock gauntlets, stun lasers, and force blasters, weapons meant to daze or disable a target, not destroy it.

Several of the Arbiter bots locked in place and looked skyward as their mouths opened wide. A static shriek emitted from their speakers before a message began to play.

"Students and faculty of Nexus academy. We are here for your technology and your service. Your deaths would be most unwelcome and tragic. Please surrender and your lives will be spared until our offer can be made. If you do not comply..." The Arbiter droids arms began to change. Some became cannons while others transformed into flamethrowers or bot casters. Others simply had plasma blades extended that they held up with clear intent. *"Then we will do what we must to accomplish the mission."*

Many of the students looked at one another, confused, angry, or frightened. Over near the bushes that decorated the entrance to the cafeteria, Indre, Izzy, Otto, and Julius stared as the security bots began to back away, clearly more focused on keeping the students safe than engaging the hostiles.

Otto noticed a lone bot only a dozen or so yards away. He slid a hand into his pants pocket, pressed a few buttons on his tablet, and caught Indre's gaze. She held down the trigger on a device in her pocket.

"To hell with this!" a voice in the crowd shouted as a student engineer—indicated by the orange band around his arm—hammered a small crowbar that he took out of his bag into the back of one of the droids' head. In one movement, he yanked it back and popped a piece of its shell off. The droid threw the student aside and turned to take aim, but before it could fire, its chest burst apart from a shot by the one Otto had taken control of.

His success was short-lived as the mechanical almost immediately turned to him and prepared an attack from its cannon, which was now aimed at the technician. Several shots came from above and it staggered long enough for Izzy to pull Otto away and the group made their escape. He looked at two small drones that attacked the droids and raised an eyebrow at Indre, who had a satisfied smile on her face.

The skirmish seemed to be enough to stir the previously stunned students into retaliation. Some attacked with whatever tools or devices they had with them while others ran to find what they could. The Arbiter droids began to fire into the crowds but most of their attacks were intercepted by the security bots who went onto the offensive to do what damage they could to hold off the onslaught.

***

"This is an emergency situation, you guys," Akello warned as Kaiden and his friends stormed outside. "It's safer for you to stay in here."

"Holy shit." Cameron yelped as the group stopped to stare at the massive ship that approached the island, along with the hail of pods that descended into the plaza and the lake.

The ace squinted and immediately recognized the armor design and colors of the droids that emerged from the pods. "Chief, are those…"

"The Arbiter droids," The EI nodded. *"Son of a bitch."*

"What is going on?" Genos asked, his eyes wide. "Are we under attack?"

"We are," Jaxon stated grimly and held a hand to his commlink. "I can't connect to the network."

All the others tried but to no avail. "They've shut it down or jammed it." Kaiden grunted and looked over to the gym. "We'll have to go and find everyone ourselves. Either follow me or stay with Akello and barricade yourself in the Animus center."

"Like hell!" Flynn shouted and he nodded at the marksman and motioned for them to follow him to the gym. Chiyo looked at Akello. "See if you can reach someone. We'll try to direct others over here for safety."

The head monitor frowned into the sky. "I'm not sure how safe the center will be," she muttered. "What would someone want with us? Other than—"

"The Animus," Chiyo stated. She clenched her fists and took one last look at the woman. "Please be safe and don't try anything foolish. We'll be back." With that, she hurried to catch up with the rest of the group as they followed Kaiden.

"Where are we going?" Cameron asked.

"The gym. Wolfson has a personal stash of weapons I can get us access to," the ace explained. "I've fought those droids and we'll need more than sticks and practice weapons to confront them."

"You've fought them?" Marlo asked. "What are they? They don't look like normal Soldier droids."

"I call them Arbiter droids. The best way to think of them is as modified Havoc droids," he explained as he pushed through the gym entrance. A few dozen students worked feverishly to take the machinery and workout stations apart to use the pieces and equipment as makeshift weapons.

"It'll be one thing dealing with the bots," Chiyo said with another glance at the enormous vessel above them. "But that ship will require more than only firepower."

"Sasha?" Wolfson bellowed into his comm. He barreled out of the R&D building with the plasma cannon Laurie had given him, charged it immediately, and fired as soon as a few of the familiar droids appeared. He turned barely in time to see one aim at him with a torch, prepared to burn him alive. In response, he raised an arm outfitted with a gauntlet of Laurie's design. A shimmering purple field enveloped it as the flames surged from its arm. The purple energy erupted from his gauntlet and enveloped both the flames and the mechanical, which began to melt as it was trapped inside the barrier with its own flames.

"Sasha, can you hear me?" he called again

"Wol...Sir..ere?" a distorted voice answered over the comms.

"Who is this?" he asked as he flipped a switch on the cannon to select its beam mode. He jerked the weapon to the side and fired to cut through a trio of bots as he made his way to the main security station.

"Wolfson, sir, are you there?" a voice crackled over the comms.

"Aye, report," Wolfson ordered and charged the gauntlet

as he rushed at a droid that approached a wounded initiate. He pounded the gauntlet into the back of the robot and the energy surged and careened the bot into the wall of the technician's dorm over forty yards away.

"I'm having trouble making contact with all available security," the guard explained as the security head helped the initiate up and turned to fire at any approaching enemy and give the student time to escape.

"They've done something to the network," he explained. "Professor Laurie is working on it as well as trying to take care of that big bastard in the sky. How were you able to get hold of me?"

"I have to connect directly to your signal, sir," the man replied. "I can't even get a team line going. The connection simply won't hold."

"Then reach out to every security team leader individually. Tell them that the students' safety is priority and all weapons are clear." Wolfson walked up to half an Arbiter droid that crawled toward him along the ground and crushed its head with a violent stamp of his boot. "And bring up Commander Sasha's signal and connect me to him if you can."

"Right away, sir. He's actually pinged his signal since this attack began. One moment."

Sasha drew a deep breath where he leaned up against the wall and finished binding the wound across his ribs seconds before his comm sparked to life. "Sasha, where the hell are you?" Wolfson demanded.

The commander looked at the lifeless bodies of the Nexus board members. His gaze settled on the corpses of Victoria and Vincent, who had killed the other members in the name of the Arbiter Organization and attempted to kill him. The fact that he was hurt but still breathing while they both had several new holes indicated that they had failed.

"Wolfson, the board is dead," he stated, glanced at the locked door behind him, and gestured for Isaac to unlock it. "Victoria and Vincent killed them, but I was able to return the favor before they could kill me. And from what I was told, Chancellor Durand may be as well."

CHAPTER ELEVEN

"The board is dead?" Wolfson muttered and the implication of the words wasn't lost on him. "And by two of their— Damn it!" Before he could finish the thought, a loud blast erupted almost a hundred yards behind him near the medics' dorm. "Are you in any danger, Sasha?"

"I was," the commander stated and approached the locked boardroom door. "Although I may be in one of the safest places in the entire school right now if what Isaac is showing me is true."

"Then do your job and show the students to your little safe place," the security head snapped and vented his cannon. "More hostiles are dropping with each passing minute—make that each second. We need backup."

Sasha tried to open the door but was met by a muffled beeping and flashing red light. "I'm currently locked in the meeting room," he replied, while Isaac immediately set to work accessing the door. "Once I'm out, I will authorize the activation of all Guardian and Soldier bots on campus. I assume Durand himself has yet to do so because—"

"He may be dead." Wolfson finished, closed the vent, and descended into a tunnel leading to the docks.

"I had hoped he was simply preoccupied with his own attack, but his death is a real possibility," Sasha agreed. "I'll head to his office personally and focus on defending and evacuating the students and personnel."

"We're on it as much as we can be, but the comms are scrambled and the emergency tunnels won't open," the security head stated and blasted a path through more arbiter droids. "I'm heading to the docks to open the ship bays and get the shuttles and boats prepped for evac. But we need those tunnels, Sasha. Find out what is jamming them."

"I assume it's the same thing that is messing with the comms and the warning systems that should have let us know about the unidentified ship headed toward our Academy," the commander retorted. "I'll let you know more once I have access to the Chancellor's console. Until then, Laurie and his team will have to do the best they can on their side. The normal rank structure has mostly disintegrated. We are in charge now, Wolfson."

"Professor!" Cyra shouted to Laurie to warn him of the approaching bots that had made their way into the structure through a maintenance system. He, however, did not look up from the dozen or so monitors he scanned through. Instead, he held a gloved hand up and a small white orb activated on a desk across from him. He gestured with his hand and the orb drifted away. She watched it disappear into a small hatch in the ceiling in the outside hallway. After a few more seconds, a large explosion was followed by a loud sizzle, then silence. She looked at the radar on her tablet as the red dots winked out almost as one.

"Cyra, I need you to head to the main offices and help to establish communication links and internal defenses," the professor requested, shut off all the monitors, and moved briskly toward the door. "I'll head up to my lab."

"Did you find the virus responsible, sir?" she asked and tried to keep pace with him. He moved at an unusually rapid pace for a man who spent most of his life in a chair behind a desk.

"I don't believe it's a simple virus," he replied and chewed a thumb as multiple thoughts raced through his mind. "Some kind of jamming device or relay is more likely. You'll have to find workarounds for now until we can destroy it."

"Is there a way to access it? Shut it down or hack it?" she asked, her hand poised near her pistol should another group of droids break in.

"I doubt that would be a better option than simply destroying it. Almost all jamming devices are basically the blunt instruments of technological warfare. They can shut down your opponent's tech but they also shut yours down. But their droids, ships, etcetera, are all working perfectly. This is something I'm not too familiar with." He spoke the last part with irritation. "It would be best to take an approach that Wolfson would advocate. I'll try to locate it and I'll need someone on the outside to eliminate it. Until then, you will need to find workarounds and defenses against the signal." He held an arm out and a holographic bracer appeared, which he ran along Cyra's tablet. "That should get us some order in this chaos for now."

"What do you need in your lab, Professor?" she asked and stopped at the elevator as Laurie headed for the stairs. "I can retrieve it while—"

"I'm trusting you with this while I focus on the other big problem we have." The door to the stairs slid open while he pointed a finger above. "Look at the sky. You can't miss it."

"Hey, Julio, turn it up!" a patron shouted and received an irate grunt from the barkeep.

"What do you want me to turn up, your midday soap operas? The monitor is basically only for ambiance anyway."

"Julio, are you blind, man?" another asked. He looked at him with confusion and frustration and finally noticed the dozens of customers all but glued to the monitor screens. "Look! The Nexus Academy is under attack by a droid army."

"What?" He snatched up the main monitor control and increased the volume on every working monitor.

"The attack continues as more capsule-shaped devices fall from the carrier above onto the Ark Academy island," the reporter stated in a voice that tried to maintain a professional calm, but tension and concern still bled through. Behind him, the newsreel displayed a scene of chaos as more pods continued to land not only on the island but also at the edges of the town behind. "Right now, Nexus has not sent out any messages and no one can make contact. Bellevue police have attempted to assist in stopping the attackers, but a number of the droids have turned their attention to the nearby city. Whether this is as a second front of the invasion or simply to keep the police force occupied, we cannot tell at this time."

Julio gaped as fires began to break out on the island and flashing laser light and explosions rocked the Academy.

His eyes widened, and he leaned against the bar for support as a hand covered his lips. "My God."

Wolfson yanked a droid off a student and ground its head under his boot. The student pointed behind him as he helped him up. He couldn't get the words out, but the security head nodded, knowing what he was trying to say. Satisfied that the younger man was now safe, he ran up the outer stairwell of the observatory to the second floor, from which he had seen him fall. He put his cannon away, exchanged it for a rifle, and held it at the ready as he reached the top and turned the corner. Three droids walked away, one in front and two behind. Those in the rear dragged a trio of students in a containment orb. Wolfson clenched his teeth and fired three shots, one through the head of each mechanical.

The two holding the orb collapsed but the shot that struck the one in front must have been off as it staggered but stretched an arm in his direction. The limb assumed the form of a cannon that immediately began to charge. It turned its head, but the security officer fired directly into the cannon barrel and ignited the blast within to demolish the robot. It was actually somewhat fortunate that the students were locked inside the containment field or they could have been caught in the blast.

He approached them quickly and flipped his gun to hold it by the barrel. The barrier was meant to be reinforced on the inside to keep those within securely trapped, but the outside was breakable with enough force. After it had been buffeted by the explosion, only a few blows from the butt of his rifle were enough to shatter it.

The three captives pushed to their feet and thanked him. He studied them quickly and realized that they were all young, probably late teens, which made them initiates. He wondered if they were prep kids. It wouldn't have made this any better, but they would at least be somewhat ready for the potential of such an attack. Still, while the idea was good, it was a different matter when they actually had to live it.

He ushered them down the stairs and took the lead. When they reached the bottom, a shaking and half-destroyed Arbiter droid hobbled over to them with its weapon raised. But before it or Wolfson could fire, two shots struck it in the head from the right. It was the student he had rescued before, holding a pistol—his pistol, he realized.

The security head raised an eyebrow as the young man ran up quickly and tried to hand it to him. "I'm sorry, sir," he stated. It seemed strange that he remembered formalities at a time like this. "The wind was knocked out of me. I should have asked but I took it before you went off so I could cover the rear—"

"It's all right, boyo," he assured him and pushed the pistol away. "You keep it for now." His gaze settled on a hatch partially hidden behind a display of flowers at the corner of the building and he beckoned the students to follow. A few others hiding in the observatory or running through the grounds saw the officer and joined them as Wolfson ran to the hatch, leaned down, and tried to pry it off. His efforts brought no success. It was still locked.

Frustrated, he sucked in a breath and glanced at another student, this one clearly a fighter as the bruises and cuts confirmed—as did the well-used droid arm in his hands repurposed as a weapon. He tossed him his rifle, took his cannon out, and instructed them to move back as he charged a shot and fired to destroy the hatch so they could gain access.

"These lead to the tunnels," he explained and made sure to provide clear instructions given the number of newbies present. "They'll take you to a safe place in town. Hurry through and tell the officials what is happening here."

"What is happening here?" one of them asked.

Wolfson sucked in a breath as he reached into a compartment on his belt. "An invasion by the Arbiter organization. And it doesn't matter if you know who they are or not. Go!" he ordered and brandished an explosive. "And take this!"

"A mine?" an initiate asked. "For what?"

"To blow the tunnel behind you of course," he told him.

"The hatch is exposed and the internal defenses are down. We cannot risk the droids using it to access the town."

"What about the other students?" a logistics student asked. "They need to escape too."

"Me and the other officers will get everyone out. All of us—every teacher and faculty member—are working to keep you safe," he vowed. "But we cannot risk—"

"I'll guard it," a red-haired soldier promised and snatched the mine from him. "I'll bring in as many students as I can and if I am overwhelmed, I'll blow the entrance to seal it."

"I'll help you," the boy with Wolfson's pistol stated and the two young men nodded to each other.

Wolfson smiled with approval. "I'll hold you boys to that. The rest of you, go now, and quickly!" With no further discussion, the group moved quickly through the opening. The security head charged his cannon and gave one last nod to the boys before he ran around the corner and fired at more droids.

With more students like that, he wouldn't have to worry about merely surviving. They'd keep this Academy from the grasping hands of the invaders.

CHAPTER TWELVE

"Captain, I don't get any responses from Command," the ensign reported and continued to work on the monitor. "There is nothing coming in from the council either."

Captain Andrion felt extremely nervous, something he shouldn't be right now. Certainly, being sent to possibly intercept a terrorist cell would make anyone anxious, but in his thirty-five years of military service, he was more accustomed to such missions than not, by this point. The aid of his Maverick-Class Battlecruiser and crew of over a hundred and fifty was also a bonus.

But sudden communication failure was always a sign of something wrong. And the fact that they could not reach either their main post or the council itself was a major problem. In addition, there was the issue that they hadn't found anyone at the coordinates—neither the terrorist cell nor allies and hell, not even an errant hiker making their way through the Russian taiga.

"Keep trying," he answered, his voice neutral but low. He looked at the helmsman. "Is there any sign of our targets?"

The man shook his head. "Nothing, sir, except for wildlife. Even the closest messenger or supply ships are more than a hundred miles away."

Andrion slumped in his chair and stroked a hand through his beard in thought. "If we get no answer from Command, we need to return at full speed. Something will have certainly—"

"Captain!" the ensign shouted and spun in his seat. "I'm getting a distress message from the council."

The captain, along with anyone else in earshot, bolted out of their seats. "What? Let me listen!"

The officer nodded, flipped a switch, and a synthetic voice spoke over the speakers.

"This is a call to all units of the World Council Military," it droned. *"The council building is currently under attack by a malicious force. All nearby military forces must return to defend the council. All military forces that are currently engaged in sensitive operations, are located more than a thousand miles away, or are unable to return due to damaged systems or an act of God, should lay low and attempt to contact emergency channels."*

"Sir?" one of the crewmen sputtered. Andrion looked back and estimated the time of day and the current schedule of Terra. It should be hovering over eastern Europe. That was more than the specified distance for a call-back, but when was the last time the council itself was attacked?

"Get the ship ready," he shouted and looked at the helmsman and crew. "We will return to Terra to assist in retaking—"

A loud blast above them cut his orders short and an alarm blared. Andrion was almost hurled to the floor when the ship shook. The crew scrambled to their seats and buckled themselves in as another explosion rocked the vessel.

"Lana, what's going on!" he shouted to the officer who worked the internal defenses.

"A breach in the ship, two—" The hull shuddered with another blast and the captain grasped the arms of his seat and pulled himself up. "Three on the starboard side in the barracks wing."

"The barracks?" he muttered and sat hastily. "Everyone, prepare for combat! Open an external and internal screen. I want to know what's going on."

"Right away, sir," one of the personnel shouted, but as they turned to bring the screen up, their monitor died and the system erupted into sparks.

"We've been hacked," another yelled as more screens faded out or systems began to malfunction.

"This is the latest Lexsys security system," one of the technicians protested. "It's not even on the market. How did they gain access without us knowing?"

Andrion thumped a button on the console of his chair and a compartment opened and revealed his rifle. He picked it up as he stood and primed it. "The same way they were able to infiltrate our ship without us knowing they were even here." He grimaced. "Lana, save what you can, activate internal security, and issue the order for lethal force."

"Understood, sir." She nodded and hurried quickly through the bridge to salvage what she could. Several techies followed her lead.

The captain found a working monitor and was able to cycle through the few remaining cameras in the barracks. Dozens of armored troops made their way in armed with cannons, machine guns, long plasma blades, and shotguns. They all wore the same thing—gray medium armor over black underlays with angled helmets. He leaned in and focused on something familiar on their suits—a stylized A with W and C beneath it. That was the insignia of the Russian Ark Academy. How did these terrorists get the suits? Was the Academy compromised?

Another shock felt closer and he braced himself against the wall as he flipped quickly through more feeds, looking for the new attack. He found it was only a couple of hundred yards from the bridge. Two pods had pounded through the hull and as the front spun open, a team of troops dropped out and began a steady approach, some with circular devices on their back.

"They are coming for the bridge," Andrion shouted and the crew hastened to their positions in preparation for the assault. He was about the pull away from the screen when he saw one final figure emerge from the pods. This one also wore the dark armor of the Ark Academy, but in addition, he wore a large armored coat of black, gold, and red. The captain gritted his teeth. He recognized it as belonging to Damyen Orlov's, the Russian Ark Academy chancellor.

The man strolled casually away as a third pod breached the ship to deliver more troops. Andrion forced himself away from the screens when he heard thuds, blasts, and screams coming from the hall.

"Sir, there are still others trapped outside and I can't activate the turrets or droids," Lana called.

"Open the doors," he ordered as he readied his rifle, and the officer looked at him in shock. "I will not hide while my ship is attacked and crew slaughtered. Open the door."

"We'll get it, sir." Two officers volunteered and hurried over to the scanners on either side to disengage the emergency lock and force the door open. As soon as it slid up, Andrion and his bridge crew fired at any of the dark armored assailants who entered their lines of fire.

"Lana!" he called as he fired at a shotgun-wielding trooper. "You have control of the bridge. As soon as the weapons get back online, find the enemy ship and destroy it."

"Yes, sir," she acknowledged, leaned around the corner, and fired a few shots from her pistol at a cluster of troops that advanced down the hall. The bullets were stopped by a shield held by one of them.

"Vanguard," Andrion muttered and gestured for those behind him to follow. "Shut the door when we all leave."

"But, sir—"

"Do it," he roared as he charged the vanguard. The enemy absorbed the shield into their gauntlets and blasted it at the captain. He fired a charged shot from his rifle at it, which canceled both out. He flipped into an alcove in the wall to shield himself as he pressed a switch on his rifle and changed to ballistic rounds. When he spun out and fired three shots, the vanguard erected a barrier, but the physical rounds passed through it and hammered the invader and two soldiers next to him. The vanguard toppled and his buddies with him.

"Push forward!" Andrion shouted and his team pushed out of the bridge. The door closed swiftly behind them He looked over to the other side of the corridor as four of his officers advanced. The grating above them gave way and two of the soldiers fell—or, rather, they were forced down as something pierced the back of their armor. The other two whirled to meet the new threat but their weapons were cut cleanly in half. A shimmer confirmed the telltale sign of a stealth generator as both his crewmen were felled. Two troops equipped with plasma blades appeared when their generators deactivated.

The captain grimaced and fired a ballistic round at the two raiders. One raised their hand and stopped the projectile in mid-air. Andiron's eyes widened as the assassin coaxed the bullet toward him before he pointed it at him and rocketed it forward as effectively as if he'd fired it from his own weapon. He dove aside as the bullet struck the wall behind him and he barely managed to escape the blast.

The two assassins engaged the remaining crew as more hostile troops flooded into the hallway. Andrion rolled to see two demolitionists at the door, preparing to blow it open. He reached for his rifle but his hand was struck before he could grab it. He looked up at a figure in a black, gold, and red jacket, who flipped the visor of his helmet up and smiled at him.

His teeth clenched, he looked into Damyen's face. "You're behind this?" He growled with barely suppressed rage. "These aren't terrorists. They're your students, aren't they?"

"They are my soldiers," the man clarified as he knelt to look the captain in the eye. "Captain...Andrion, isn't it?" he asked. "You can make this easier on your crew by surrendering and giving the order to stand down. We'll take this ship, but you get to decide how long it will take." He retrieved a small device and held it up to the captain's mouth as he gestured to the speakers above them. "And how long the clean-up will be."

He wanted to spit at the traitor, but he caught another sight of the demolitionists, ready to blow the bridge door. They merely waited for Damyen to give the order. More screams issued from above him and around him. How many were there left to save?

With a solemn sigh, he nodded. The enemy leader's smile grew wider as he pressed the button on the device. "This is Captain Andrion," the captain began. "To the crew of the *Heimdallr*, lay down your arms and surrender."

Damyen looked around and listened for further sounds of battle. The ship became eerily quiet. He nodded, placed the device in his pocket, and reached to his belt. "Good choice, Captain. Certainly, a better one than the other captains made."

"Other captains?" he asked. "How many—"

"You make the fifth," he stated as he drew a pistol and placed it against his head. "If it counts, this was easily the biggest ship yet."

Andrion looked at the pistol and strained under the man's foot to reach his rifle. "You said you would—"

"Make it easier on your crew. Their deaths will be much faster this way," Damyen told him with a sick laugh. "Except the Ark graduates. They will live and they'll even have a place." The chancellor's finger eased down on the trigger. "As one of my soldiers."

CHAPTER THIRTEEN

K aiden rushed to the back of the arena in Wolfson's training area. He shoved tables aside as he searched frantically for something.

"Kaiden, are you looking for the weapons rack?" Marlo asked and pointed behind him.

"No, I'm— Actually, that's not a bad idea. Genos, deactivate the lock on that, would you, while I—aha!" He shoved a locker aside and yanked up the mat to reveal two doors beneath it. Quickly, he crouched and slid a small window open to reveal a keypad into which he punched several numbers. A small circle appeared when he pressed confirm. "Marlo, grab the other handle."

The demolitionist nodded. The ace grasped the right handle of the vault and Marlo the left. When the keypad blinked green, Kaiden nodded and they both pulled the heavy doors of the vault open to a small space beneath with a ladder.

"What is that?" Flynn asked and peered down. "It's pitch-black down there."

"The light switch is in the storage room." Kaiden slid through the hole, his hands on the ladder. "It's kind of cramped down there. Amber and Chiyo, do you mind coming down? I'll hand stuff up to you."

"It had better be good stuff," Cameron commented.

The ace grinned at the bounty hunter before his head disappeared into the hole. "This is Wolfson's personal stash. He showed it to me after Gin's attack, just in case."

"This is certainly a case." Flynn nodded and gestured to the two women. "Get down there!"

Kaiden reached the storage room, turned the light on, and hurriedly began to grab any weapons or device he could and handed them to Amber, who handed them to Chiyo, who distributed them to the others in the group.

"There's enough down here to arm all of us," he shouted as he placed a rifle and a container of shock grenades in Amber's hands. "Genos and Jaxon, take the weapons on the practice rack and give them to the students out in the gym."

"I've unlocked the rack, friend Kaiden," Genos responded. "But you know that many of these are training weapons, correct?"

"You're an engineer, right? Can you see the safety mods on the guns?" he asked. "If you disengage them, they are normal guns. They might not be the best quality but are better than nothing. We'll try to share the leftovers from in here but we'll need all the help we can to get into the security facility."

"Security?" Jaxon asked. "What are you looking for there?"

"Codes to the armory," he stated. He threw the

remaining weapons into a pack and placed it on his back. Amber and Chiyo scrambled out to give him room as he ascended again. "Wolfson told me that's where he keeps my shock pistol stored since I don't walk around with it— dumbass that I'm feeling right about now."

"Won't the security forces be able to open it for us?" Amber asked.

"Maybe, if there are any nearby. But my guess is that most if not all of them are out there being security." He tossed an extra bag to Jaxon, who nodded and helped Genos pack the remaining weapons as the mechanist had carefully slid the safety mods out and placed them on a small tray he had found from one of the tables Kaiden flipped over.

"I assume by the name that's where all the guns are kept?" Cameron asked.

"Most of them." The ace nodded and tossed him a container of net grenades. "There are stashes of guns all over the island, this being a military academy and all. But that's where all the good ones are. I believe in my fellow comrades and all that—"

"But you'd believe in them more if they had real fire-power?" Flynn finished and received a nod in confirmation.

"I...can't join you," Amber muttered almost in a whisper.

"What's up Amber?" Marlo asked.

Flynn looked at her with concern. "Medbay?" he asked. and she nodded as she activated her sub-machine gun. "Her mother—we have to check on her."

Kaiden nodded. "Right, Dr. Soni...and everyone." He

listened to the fighting outside. "I'm worried about all of them too. Do what you need to do and get everyone you can to safety."

The marksman nodded and glanced quickly at Marlo, who placed a shotgun on his back. "We'll go with her and will join up with you again when we're done."

The ace looked at Chief. "Can you keep a line up?"

"I've been tinkerin'," the EI stated. *"I can keep one channel open efficiently. But there is something screwy going on, partner. Whatever is taking hold of the tech on the island isn't only a virus or simple hackery."*

"I'm sure Laurie is all over that," he replied and selected a pistol—slim, rapid-fire, and with a good core, it still felt light compared to Debonair. He grimaced. All his gear was with Julio and he couldn't get a call out. Part of him hoped the barkeep would find a way to bring his gear and loads of other presents to him, but with that big bastard in the sky, it would be suicide.

He placed the pistol in his jacket pocket, clipped a container of shocks and a container of thermals on his belt, and picked up a machine gun. "Chief will stay in contact with you, Flynn. Y'all be safe."

"Same to you, mate," Flynn replied and he, Amber, and Marlo headed to the door. Jaxon handed them the pack of training weapons to give to the others as he and Genos walked over to Kaiden.

"So our plan is to head to security, then?" the Tsuna ace asked as he chose a machine gun and rifle for himself.

"Will Officer Wolfson be present?" Genos asked, picked up a small box of gadgets, and rummaged through it.

"I've yet to reach him," Kaiden said and glanced at

Chief, who merely shook from side to side. "We may run into him, but I won't rely on chance. We need to get into his office. He'll have the current access code to the armory in his desk."

"Will we simply blast our way in?" Cameron asked as he twirled a shotgun.

"I have a spare key," the ace said and held a blue access card up. "He hides it in the bear figurine next to the door and I snagged it on the way in."

"The head officer has really grown to trust you over the years, hasn't he?" Chiyo asked.

He looked at the key before he slid it into his pants pocket and ruffled his hair. "I guess so. It's a good thing too considering the circumstance."

"How will we alert the other students about the available weapons with the comms down?" Jaxon asked.

Kaiden retrieved his tablet from his other pocket. "The emergency channel is still running," he stated.

"If we can access the security console, we can change the message and get it out to all the students," Chiyo summarized.

He put the tablet away and readied his rifle. "Assuming this problem with the tech doesn't get worse. Let's get going before it does, yeah?"

The group looked at each other and nodded, all ready to return to the chaos but this time, prepared to fight rather than run.

Durand was in bad shape. His breathing was labored, his

head was bleeding, and the left side of his chest had been burned by laser fire. His hands shook as he pulled himself behind the desk. He readied his pistol when he heard metallic steps at the doorway. Another of the droids stepped inside and scanned the room while the chancellor held the trigger down to charge the blast. It must have sensed the increasing energy of the pistol as it surged forward and knocked the desk aside. He rolled over and fired the blast directly into its chest. It staggered and he produced his plasma blade and stabbed it into the blast point to slice through and into its core.

The Arbiter droid revealed its own blade and lashed out at the chancellor. He fell back but the weapon cut deep into his chest and he lurched into the wall behind him and slid down. His blade fell from the robot's chest, having apparently cut deep enough as the lights in its eyes dulled and darkened and it toppled.

Unfortunately, three more moved into the room.

He drew a deep, ragged breath as he vented his pistol and closed his eyes. One of the droids held its arm cannon up, ready to fire. He heard three shots, felt nothing, and opened his eyes to gape at the holes in the chests of the three mechanicals. They sputtered for a moment before they fell and a figure in a black jacket stepped over them.

Despite the pain and blurred vision, he recognized his rescuer immediately. "Sasha…" he whispered in a croaking voice.

"Chancellor, I'm sorry I wasn't here sooner," the commander stated, slung his rifle over his back, and knelt at his side.

"I should feel sorry for the fact that I could only handle

nine of those bastards." Durand sighed and held his head. "My secretary, Teresa, was a double agent. Can you believe it?"

"As were board members Victoria and Vincent," Sasha told. "The rest of the board is dead, sir."

"Son of a bitch." He hissed in pain as the commander helped him to lean up. When he coughed, small specks of blood appeared in his hand that both men saw.

"Sasha, hand me your tablet," he stated. He did so and Durand retrieved his own which had been only slightly damaged in the fight. "Franklin, give Sasha Chevalier chancellor status."

"Durand?" the commander questioned but the man ignored him.

"This is obviously an emergency situation, but I still need the code, sir," the chancellor's EI stated.

Durand nodded. "Code 01350, chancellor authorization password: Magenta Skies." He chuckled as the EI began to transfer all the authority of the chancellorship to Sasha. "Magenta Skies was where I planned to retire in a few years. I only changed the password a few months ago."

"Sir, I have some medical supplies I can—"

"If I remove this arm across my chest, I'll bleed out before you can apply the gel," he muttered, his voice a little weaker. "Sasha, do what needs to be done to keep these students safe, understand?"

The commander pursed his lips and nodded. "I do, sir. I will make sure that this is not the end of the Academy."

"Such commitment." Durand laughed as he looked down to confirm that the transfer had completed. "Coming from someone...who was hesitant to join...in the first place."

Sasha steadied him to stop him sliding to the side. "I'm glad I came, and it didn't take long for me to feel this way."

The chancellor rolled his head back against the wall and released a long breath. "Make sure to remember that...as you take the Academy back," he said, his voice faint. "Feeling like that...those bonds and memories..." His words faltered and he took short, minute breaths. "That's what...keeps the fire...going."

The commander nodded, took the other man's tablet, and stood. He saluted the fallen chancellor before he turned to assume his new responsibilities.

CHAPTER FOURTEEN

"One…two…three!" Mack and Luke heaved against the door to the engineers' bay but were only knocked back by their effort and almost tumbled into Raul.

"These aren't rusted, dilapidated doors, you oafs," the tracker huffed. "Most of the academy is in lockdown so the engineering bay wouldn't be any—"

"She'll get it open," Silas called, and the trio looked at him where he walked beside a girl in an engineer's orange jumpsuit and with her brown hair tied back. She pushed past the group and over to a terminal at the door they had attempted to break.

"Who's she?" Mack asked as the raider helped to pull him up.

"An actual engineer, for one thing," Silas explained as he moved out of the way so Raul could help Luke. "But she's also an assistant to one of the workshop teachers. She has the emergency codes for the bay and several other rooms."

"Really?" Luke asked and punched a fist into his hand excitedly. "We're finally making some progress."

"Silas told me you guys were looking for weapons," the engineer added as the terminal she accessed activated and she began to punch the code in. "I said that we don't really keep many weapons on hand here in the workshops—"

"But you do have tools," Raul replied. "And heavy-duty ones as well."

"They might not be practical or professional," Mack admitted, and the group glanced hastily toward the entrance as a blast went off that sounded really close to the building. "But we'll take anything, at this point."

"The others agreed with that," she concurred. The terminal beeped when it accepted the code and the door opened for the group.

"The others?" Luke asked as Silas made his way inside.

"I found her and a few others barricaded in a room down the hall," he explained. "When I told them what we were trying to do, a few of them decided to head to another department to get at the tools and gadgets in there."

"So we actually have a force ready to fight these guys?" Mack asked and his grin widened.

"My friends are mostly engineers and techies," the girl explained as she searched through some of the drawers in the classroom. "They can fight and know some tricks, but they won't be able to stand toe to toe alongside you soldiers."

"Hmm, right now, we're all soldiers." Raul picked up a long staff with prongs at the end. He pressed a switch and sparks jumped from the prongs in a sudden burst. While he didn't know what it was used for normally, he definitely had a new use for it.

"I'm sure everyone was caught off guard and some probably still are," Luke reasoned as he examined a large gauntlet. He recognized it as a larger version of the one he normally saw Genos wear when they were training. "Anyone able and willing to fight will be a big help."

"That's why I didn't try to stop them," Silas admitted as he retrieved a soldering gun. He checked the inside and nodded when he saw that it had been tinkered with and the maximum output was more than a little past the safe number. Still, he would have to get quite close to use it.

"Does anyone have a plan for when we get out of here?" Mack asked. He slid his hand into a gauntleted vice claw and tested it.

"Round up who we can and see if we can get our hands on some real weapons," Silas suggested.

"We need to focus on getting off the island," the engineer protested, and her composure seemed to slide a little. "Even if you find proper weapons, you can't actually fight them. I've already seen bodies on the ground and other students being taken away—"

"Taken?" Raul asked and all four of them looked sharply at her. "Taken where?"

She managed to calm the moment of fear and took a deep breath. "I'm...I'm not sure, but I saw some of the students being taken in either nets or barriers."

"Which direction?" Silas asked.

"Towards the north-west part of the island, I think. Although I don't know what for."

Mack stroked his chin thoughtfully and glanced at Silas. "The only thing in that direction besides the logistics dorms and some of the workshops is the docks."

The raider nodded. "If they are trying to take their hostages somewhere, they'll need a place to pick them up."

"I guess we have a destination." Luke grunted and held his gauntlet up. "Although isn't that where the security forces have their headquarters? Those bots will have to face the most well-armed and trained guys on the island."

"I'm sure many of them are spread around the Academy," Silas countered and a concerned frown slid onto his face. "And even if a number of them make it back, there are more than enough droids they'll have to deal with."

Indre popped the back of the pistol open and ejected the ID chip before she slid her bypass chip in and waited for the weapon to unlock. She looked toward the cafeteria, where she had taken the weapon from the side of the fallen security officer. The picture of his twisted body rose in her mind, but she put it aside when she heard a beep. Quickly, she removed the bypass chip, closed the pistol, and tossed it to Izzy before she worked on the rifle.

The scout snatched the pistol out of the air and in almost the same motion, fired several shots at a nearby droid with low shields. It turned in her direction, but she simply focused her fire on its chest and finally felled it when its chest armor melted away. Sparks spat from the metal body as it collapsed.

She and Indre swapped weapons when the rifle was unlocked. Close by, Otto worked on something in his holo-screen. "Can you make contact with anyone?"

"I have my EI working on that," he stated and remained

focused on the screen. "I'm trying to get access to the plaza's main terminal so I can get into the security functions."

"What for?" Izzy asked and noticed another two droids coming down the alley. She signaled Indre and both women turned and fired a volley that drove the mechanicals back. Otto continued to work unperturbed.

"Turrets, barricades, drone deployment, emergency hatches to the tunnels—does none of that ring a bell?" he asked. "Those are some of the things that are supposed to appear in this kind of situation. They told us that every time we had a safety seminar, yet I don't see any of them." He looked up for a brief moment as if to remind himself of the situation before he returned his attention to the screen and continued his efforts. "There must be something wrong with the automatic detection and the connection to the main center. I had hoped that I was close enough to access it remotely, but it looks like I need to get to the node itself if I want a chance of doing anything."

"I think you'll have to pocket that idea for later, Otto," Julius said in a strained voice. The group looked over to where the medic helped a security officer over to the wall and rested him against it. Julius took out a small container, unlatched it, and opened it to reveal several small vials. "This will help with the pain and get you back on your feet," he said, his voice calm and reassuring as he unclasped the officer's chest piece to apply the gel to the wound on his ribs. "It's a good thing you had a divided plate. That helps defend against bladed weaponry."

The man nodded and winced a little as the gel was

applied. "Still, that plasma blade was hotter than even the latest models. Nothing we have could stop it."

"The shielding didn't do much either." The biologist looked at Indre. "Have you ever heard of plasma blades with dissonance mods?"

"It's not unheard of but they don't last long. The type of material they use for plasma blades doesn't work well with the vibrations," she explained and vented her pistol. "Whatever they are using isn't simply a shoddy mod job."

Otto sighed and closed his holoscreen. "You said I should save my idea for later, Jul?" He crouched even lower and craned his neck to look at his friend. "Does that mean you think we won't be able to hold them off?"

"I don't," Julius stated and assisted the security officer to stand. "But that doesn't mean we can't fight back later. For now, Officer Malcolm has told me of a hatch nearby with a manual lock. If we can reach that and open it, that's another opportunity to help save our fellow students."

Izzy looked at Indre, who nodded and shut the vent of her pistol. "It's better than simply sitting here and waiting for them to come to us."

"I had similar thoughts." The biologist turned to the officer. "Are you all right?"

"I still feel a burn but the pain isn't crippling anymore," the man assured him, now able to stand without support. "What brand is that?"

"My own proprietary blend—trade secret," he replied as he stowed the vial. "When we get out of here, I have a feeling I'll have to make much more of it."

CHAPTER FIFTEEN

A cruiser floated silently above the clouds outside Rome with a light-refracting shield activated that made it virtually invisible to anyone below. The lights pulsed and shined for brief moments along the shields before they were swallowed again by the twisting winds as the vessel hovered above the mountains.

A figure stood on the bridge of the ship and contemplated the beautiful city below him. He dreamed of it being the place where he would set up the first official branch of the future Arbiter council. It was a fitting choice. Centuries before, this was once the greatest city on earth, a marvel of human knowledge and achievement. Maybe, once the strife was over and they succeeded in keeping mankind alive, the world would look at the city with that kind of amazement once again.

He wondered if the news had reached Rome yet. Terra was only a few countries away, by this point, and while his subordinates had made sure to cut communication off, the news would have to travel quickly, wouldn't it? An errant lobbyist might have left the council building before the attack and should have escaped the area by now, made a call, and let the world know. Perhaps his comrades were too thorough for that.

Paranoia crept over him and he reminded himself that they had so much at stake.

The mental hoops that people would jump through to retain their sense of normalcy as the world shifted around them were almost as admirable as they were idiotic. Although those were merely signs, minor effects of the chaos they could simply shrug off, it was another thing to see it and so few could. They didn't have his vision.

The figure withdrew into the ship and walked the corridors. He recalled buying it as a gift to himself—so long ago, now. The previous owner was unknown and the craft had been found abandoned in a forest. Such a waste, most thought, as this model had been top-of-the-line forty years before. Merrick agreed with that and had found it a shame that he couldn't get the previous owner to part with it for credits or trade.

He entered his study, dimly lit by glow strips and mood lighting. A large stage for the screen stood empty with only a few seats in front of it. He walked onto the platform and moved past large stacks of books, notes, and old maps that had been strewn about. All were antiques that many people would treasure from an age long forgotten, but they were no more than simple tools to him—and inconvenient ones at that. He wasn't there for them right now and instead, he sat, took his tablet out, and placed it on the desk beside him.

His journal was filled with pages upon pages of

personal anecdotes and records. With an empty page open, he began to speak.

"Subject number four hundred and forty-one. Name, Tessa Hart." As he spoke, his words recorded themselves on the tablet screen. "She seemed the gentle sort, or perhaps at one point she was before the serum got ahold of her." When he leaned back in his chair, it groaned with age and he ignored it and rested his chin upon his palm. He closed his eyes and thought back. "It's a pity really. She could have made a fantastic bride for the right man or woman. However, the price of science can be high. She knew this but the real tragedy was that it could have been prevented. Because I had failed so long ago—"

Merrick's tablet glowed and an alert appeared in the corner to indicate that a door had opened at the front of the ship along with a warning that a storm was brewing outside. "I intend to right that mistake soon. The mission has begun in earnest and we should have all the vital points under our control within a few months. Although, if we are successful at the Nexus Academy and if I can get my hands on the original—the one I should have taken with me once I was replaced... That is a moment I will always recall, when I was ousted for not agreeing to the council's vision. When they heard my plea about what I had seen and told me that I was compromised—" Footsteps could be heard down the hall, approaching his study. He straightened and flipped the tablet. "That was the moment when I realized that I alone may have to save this planet of fools."

A new member of the crew approached, clad head to foot in black but wearing an ashen hooded poncho. She strode to the foot of the stage, stopped directly in front, and bowed to him. He stood from his chair, crossed over to the left side of the stage, and descended the stairs.

"Good evening, sir," said the hooded one in a monotone rasp as she straightened from her gesture of respect.

"Good evening, Leda," he replied with a nod. He stood in front of her. She remained unmoving save for her index finger that rubbed against her thumb, a nervous habit. "Your modifications were a wise decision, Leda. Jensen wished for me to pass on his regards for the work."

"Thank you, sir, it was a simple transfer of—" She stopped herself as she let her hood drop and gazed at him with one emerald eye and one glowing blue one. Her auburn hair fell to the nape of her neck. "It was my pleasure. I only wanted to apologize for not thinking of it sooner. It could have thrown the entire mission into disarray."

The man walked around her as she spoke and shook his head.

"You went through all the trouble to stay up for many nights on end and work to make sure the droids were at their best. I must say I did not see such a fire in you when the droids at the Fenrir facility were destroyed." He turned to look directly into her eyes and his brow creased with the intensity he felt. "What will be accomplished today, tomorrow, and in the coming months will be because of you, because you had a gift you were willing to share with me. That has allowed me to give the gift of salvation to the rest of the world."

Leda was beside herself and her thumb glided across her fingers "I... Well... Certainly, sir, you know I like a good challenge," she said somewhat bashfully and seemed to recognize the childish nature of the reply. Merrick smiled and laughed. She believed it to be in response to her silly statement, but he was constantly amused by her naivety. Not only that, she was quite smitten with him and he obliged her fantasies from time to time.

But he had a reality to bring to fruition.

"Ah, there it is—the same passion that piqued my curiosity so very long ago. I began to wonder if it had all but left you. I personally see no use for someone who has no spirit in them There is nothing to enrich…" He ceased his slow circle around her and looked at the single window in the room. A few drops of rain spattered against it. He finished his statement with a quiet whisper only he could hear. "And nothing to break." He slid his hand into a satchel that was clipped to his waist, took one of Leda's hands, and placed a small glass cube in her palm. It contained a glowing orb and she examined it curiously, not entirely sure what it was.

"You'll be needed at the general's side soon," he told her and moved toward his chair. She looked at the cube with trepidation as her mind raced with possibilities and fears. "If everything goes according to plan, you'll have a new project. And if it does not, you'll have a different one." He focused his gaze on her, smiled, and pointed at the device. "Please do try to keep hold of that. It's currently the only one we have."

"What is it, sir?" she asked and frowned at it. Her artificial eye narrowed as she examined it again.

"What do you think it is?" he asked teasingly as he sat and tilted his head while he watched for her reaction. "I'm curious as to whether you can guess."

Leda held the cube in her hand. "It seems like some kind of containment device...but also a computer? It has the properties of one. But if there is no way to access it, I assume it needs to be connected to another device. But what would you need to contain that would require an operating..." Her voice trailed off and a small smile formed on her lips.

"I see it's coming together." Merrick chuckled. "I'm sorry it took so long, but you will finally have your chance to examine the professor's achievement, although it may not be the one I had promised you before."

The woman hid the cube in her poncho and gave him a short bow. "Either one will suffice sir, but if it's his personal one, that won't have the same benefits and potential as the soldier's EI."

"We'll get the other one sooner or later." He leaned back in his chair and picked his tablet up. "I know I've been saying that for years, but that time is coming soon. For now, make your way to the transporter. I've contacted the general and he will have someone port you over."

She straightened quickly and nodded, left the study silently, and walked to the transporter room. The truth was that she wasn't a fan of the tech. It was only a decade old which made it still too new in her opinion, and there was still the chance of— No, she would not focus on that. This was Merrick's wish and she would obey

The AO leader looked at what had been typed and saved the log for another occasion. This journal was him simply catching up and the incident he had referred to had happened several years before. He checked the feeds from his various sites—the WC building, Damyen's ship, and battles in Australia, India, Japan, and Brazil. The attacks in France and Finland should start fairly soon.

He closed his eyes and his thoughts once again returned to the mission—or, at least, he tried to focus on that. Instead, he saw a terrifying visage of a beast surrounded by the stars whose light distorted and swirled around it as it stretched toward him and his planet. Merrick drew a deep breath and leaned forward. That image had haunted him for decades, but it also drove him.

CHAPTER SIXTEEN

Wolfson ran out of an alley and flipped the switch on his cannon to return it to charge mode. He held the trigger down as he neared the front of the security building. The sounds of battle increased as he moved closer to the most well-armed building on the island. It would appear that he was not the only one to realize how important the security center was to the fight right now, and not the only one on either side, unfortunately.

Security forces and droids clashed with Arbiter bots. Students either joined the fray or weaved through the chaos to find a safer passage. The security head glanced at the edge of the building, where a tunnel had been opened. Those running through the battle were trying to reach it. There were more than four dozen tunnels and exits off the island and yet this was only the second one he actually saw open. The priority was to get the system working again or at least deactivate the automated locks to let others through. The docks would have to wait for now.

He raised his cannon and fired at a cluster of droids

that pursued a group of scrappy students in torn and bloody uniforms. The blast destroyed the mechanicals and he yelled at the students to pick up the pace and that he would hold the enemy back. No sooner had the promise left his lips than another droid came up behind him for the kill. It stopped short, however, when lasers burrowed through its skull and he stepped aside as it collapsed. He looked over at a team of seven security officers who emerged from the same alley he had just run through. Six of them fanned out and began to assist the other forces against the bots while another ran up to him. He noted the tag on the chest plate. He remembered training Officer Haldt personally when he'd joined them but hadn't seen him much during the last few years after he assumed the role of police liaison. This was one hell of a time for reintroductions.

"Head Officer," the man yelled, probably because the mic on his helmet had been damaged. "Are you here to look into the situation with the emergency hatches too, sir?"

Wolfson nodded, held his cannon up, and fired to his left at two droids that crawled up from the water at the side of the island. "Aye. The professor is looking into taking care of whatever is disabling the majority of our automated defenses but we can still work with the hardware itself. If we flip a couple of switches, we'll have the tunnels open and can work on getting the students out."

"The Academy is lost then?" Haldt asked before he noticed a bot drop to the ground behind the giant, prepared to leap at him. He raised his rifle. "Sir!"

The head officer didn't even look back and simply

swung his gauntlet arm back to thrust the mechanical away. He stormed over to it and began to pound it repeatedly. "Some buildings are lost," Wolfson roared with another stamp of his boot. "And it's only temporary. The Academy is these students. And whoever the asshole is behind this—and I have a good guess who it is—they want the students."

Wolfson knocked the droid's body off his foot and turned. "Listen closely. Head to the docks and get the boats and ships ready. I'll handle getting the hatches open." He grinned, glanced at his belt, and unclipped a device. Haldt recognized it as an old radio device—an antique by modern standards—but when the head officer passed it to him, he understood why he had it. "It's already on the right channel, sir?"

"Of course!" He put his cannon away and drew his shotgun. "Contact me when you have the hangars and bay under control or at least ready to go. I'll send a signal out on the emergency band to let the students know they can leave either by the tunnels or ships."

The man nodded and saluted. "Understood, sir!"

The head officer looked up, raised his shotgun, and fired at a bladed droid. "Formalities later—get movin'."

Haldt nodded, rounded his team up, and ran toward the docks while Wolfson turned to the security building and bellowed with rage as he charged into the battle.

Marlo forced the doors to the medbay apart. Amber had taken one of the side paths through the auditorium in the hope that there would be less resistance. Technically, that had been the case, but only because the enemy forces had apparently already been through.

In the hall lay dozens of broken, fried droids, both enemy and security. Amber noticed two bodies and grimaced. Both were security officers and had several long cuts across their chests. They weren't even wearing armor—they possibly didn't have time to put it on. Her gaze scanned the room and located another body, this one familiar with gray skin and a rounded head. It was Dr Mortis, the Mirus transfer. There were three deep wounds from kinetic rounds in his chest. From the way he had fallen near one of the hallway doors and the fact that she saw a pistol beside him, she realized that he had tried to hold the forces off for others.

"Amber, do you know where your mom might be?" Marlo asked and leaned around the corner. "I can't hear anything—no footsteps or laser fire. It's quiet in here."

"There are panic rooms for emergencies," Flynn suggested quickly as if to erase the potential implications of what Marlo said. "They are well-defended against anything but high-level cannon and explosives. I think they are even shielded against several types of artificial vision. The droids could walk right past them in that case."

"Maybe..." Amber said quietly, straightened, and held her weapon up. "Let's stay close together. We'll have to check each of the rooms individually."

"Roger. I'll take point." Marlo stepped over a mound of robotic parts into the next hallway.

Flynn ran up and placed a hand on the demolitionist's shoulder. "Are you sure, mate? You're not suited up."

The large man nodded and gave him a small grin. "I don't know much else and I'm still the biggest target anyway."

The trio walked through the halls and encountered only more destruction and rooms torn apart. Flynn noticed small grooves in the floor with drops of blood inside. Someone had been dragged away by the look of them and tried to claw themselves free.

Amber kept a lookout for any survivors, perhaps even some who tried to play dead. It wasn't a tactic that would work against robots that could read a heart rate, but in desperate times, people were likely not to think about their plans when in a panic. Unfortunately, every organic body she saw only presented another look at death. She was accustomed to the sight—they all were in their own ways—but seeing the medbay staff, people she was familiar with and worked with, some of whom she even considered close friends... They had yet to find those friends, and guilt nagged at the relief she felt as she walked amongst the dead.

Marlo held a hand up as they neared another turn. He looked around and motioned for the other two to join him. They did so and peeked out at a pair of Arbiter droids staring at a door.

The three teammates leaned back behind the wall. The demolisher held his up tablet with a message. *What are they doing?*

Flynn shrugged, retrieved his own tablet and typed, *Is that a panic room?* for Amber to read.

She shook her head and made a trigger motion with her fingers to tell him to eliminate them. The marksman nodded and stowed his tablet as Marlo stepped aside and let him get into position. He took aim from a slight angle, found the perfect point, and fired to shoot both mechanicals through the head in one shot.

"They don't have shields," he noted as he lowered his rifle. "Something must be messing with them."

"Let's see what's behind the door." The demolisher jogged over to it and knocked. "Is anyone in there?"

There was no answer at first, so Flynn took his tablet out, wrote a message, and held it against the glass on the side of the door. Hopefully, whoever was in there could see it, assuming someone was in there, of course.

After a few moments, the door unlocked. Marlo took the handle and slid it open slowly, his weapon at the ready. "We're Nexus students. Who's in here?"

"Dr. Abar, Nexus scientist in the exotech division," a voice called.

"Dr. Abar, it's me—Amber Soni!" the battle medic responded. When he heard her voice, he stumbled out and threw his arms open.

"Amber, you're safe!" he said, his voice a mixture of relief and fear.

"Do you know what was up with those droids, Doctor?" Flynn asked. "They simply stood there like they were in rest mode or something."

He nodded and slid a hand into his coat pocket. "A technician came in with burns yesterday from an accident and left this device." He revealed a small orb to them, black with white glowing lines. "I meant to return it to him this afternoon, before this…invasion. Droids raced through the halls. I had the device on me and when I stumbled and fell during the attack, I activated it by accident. I was worried it was some kind of explosive for a second, but instead, any bots that were within a few yards of me walked right past me. It cloaks me somehow—or did. I think it's damaged or running out of power. They still didn't attack me, but they started to pursue me while I tried to meet up with Doctor —" Abar's eyes widened and he grasped Amber by the shoulders. "Did you come through the front?"

"No, through the back entrance and the Auditorium building," she answered.

The doctor's face paled and an expression of panic set in. "Your mother—Dr. Soni—she's barricaded with the remaining personnel and injured in the ICU. The droids couldn't get through the barriers, but I saw some headed toward the maintenance room. The ICU becomes a makeshift bunker during a lockdown, but to do that, they have to lock and shield the vents and rely on an oxygen supply. If the droids gain access to the interior systems of the medbay, they could suffocate them."

The group prepared to leave quickly. "Which way?" Flynn cried as Amber spun toward the door.

"Down the hall and to the right. I'll take point!" she stated.

"Wait!" Abar shouted before the group left the room and threw the device to her. "I'll find a way out on my own. If you can make use of that, please do."

She nodded and slid it into a pouch at her belt. "Thank you and be careful, Doctor," she replied as the three ran out to save Dr. Soni, the staff, and the patients from the waiting horde.

CHAPTER SEVENTEEN

Kaiden, his team, and around twenty students armed from the gym barreled out of the doors and fired wildly at the droids that attempted to gain access. Some began to yell with excitement as they finally took the fight to their attackers but several loud bangs behind them interrupted the impromptu war cries. Many turned as droids dropped into the gym from above, having broken in from the roof.

"Shit, get back there," the ace shouted at some of the other students as he continued to fire, keeping the droids at bay. Several of the group broke off the retaliatory offensive to help the students still taking shelter inside.

"Kaiden, the sky is clearing," Chiyo stated calmly as she vented her sub-machine gun and switched it with her pistol. "The pods are slowing down."

His gaze darted up for a few seconds and it seemed that she was right. The number of containers filled with mechanical death had significantly decreased and he only noticed a few more making landfall. When he looked at the large group of droids ranged against them like a living-dead horde and the dozens of containers he could see scattered across the island, however, he knew better than to be too hopeful.

"Watch ou—ah!" a student cried when their chest was struck with an electrified spike that threw them into spasms as they fell. Kaiden whipped around and shot the droid that had fired the shot as two other students helped pull the wounded one inside the gym.

That was when he realized that they weren't firing their cannons, lasers, or kinetic rounds at them. In fact, they weren't even armed with blades. The droids were firing non-lethal objects—shock pins like the one that wounded the soldier, net grenades, and trap barriers. A Tsuna soldier nearby struggled on the ground as a metal bola-like device had caught her by the legs. He ran over, drew the heat blade, and activated it to help the Tsuna, who fought to free herself. "Sorry, all I have is a heat blade," he stated, knelt quickly, and sliced into the wires.

"I'll take the damaged skin over being a hostage," she replied and forced her legs apart as he finished severing the metal. The Tsuna stood and looked across the plaza. "They broke my rifle, I'm sorry."

The ace shook his head and handed her his spare pistol. "Don't worry about it. You need to help the others in the gym."

She took the gun and nodded. "Understood. Where will you go?"

"We'll head to the security facility." The two moved to

the entrance and he could see his group beginning to break away. "We're trying to get more weapons and unlock the emergency tunnels. If you can, see if you can head to the acquisitions department. They will have some weapons there as well—assuming it hasn't already been raided by now."

"We'll keep it in mind," she promised, turned, and fired at a retreating droid. "Thank you for giving us a fighting chance. Now go!"

He nodded, jogged past his team, and tapped them on the way to signal that it was time for them to move in earnest.

"Professor, we have the mainframe online but we cannot activate the connection without fixing the power issue," one of the more than a dozen technicians in the lab exclaimed. Laurie looked at the alpha EI relay—a copy, actually, based on his father's design. It would allow him to find any EI in the world assuming he had its ID number. Or, in this case, with a little tinkering, allow him to access the onboard EI of the ship above the Academy and shut that damn thing down.

Ominous sounds of destruction below drew closer as the arbiter droids made their way deeper into the facility. They were running short of time. He didn't know if these mechanicals were there to take them prisoner or kill them, and he didn't have the time to consider which might potentially be worse right now.

"Jonas, Kaley, position the remaining droids and drones at the ready," he ordered and walked up to the central monitor on the relay. "Gustav, shut the power down in all nonessential facilities, including the experimentation wing and my personal office. I guess I'll simply have to hope this madness is over in time for my wine to still be properly chilled."

Gustav nodded. "Understood, sir, but we'll still need more. There's trouble with the relay already as it is since we modified it. Combining that with the interference we need to—"

"Get that damn thing destroyed!" Laurie yelled and pounded a fist against the console. "My apologies. It is a tense situation. The biggest energy draw is the emergency defense system and we certainly cannot shut that down. Prepare to activate the supplementary core cooling system and overclock it."

The technician hesitated but he knew that would be the only way to get the surplus of power they needed in those particular circumstances. "Right, sir."

"We need to discover where that damn device is!" Laurie growled his frustration. "It has to be on the island somewhere—perhaps made its way here with the bots. But I don't know how we'll find it without some kind of radar."

"Gah!" Kaiden shouted as his head began to pound. He came to a sudden stop and almost toppled but was able to stumble behind the walls of the technician's workshop building before he fell to his knees with his hands around his head.

"Kaiden! What's wrong?" Genos asked, looked away from the fighting for a moment, and came to his friend's aid.

"My head feels like it's melting." He grunted and clenched his teeth. "Shit, not again. I'm not even in the Animus."

"I recognize this feeling," Chief stated, and his voice shifted between clear and fuzzy. *"Back at Ramses—that emitter they used on us."*

He winced as he forced himself up. "Didn't we stop them from taking it?"

"The device, but that assassin ran off with that little drive, which probably had the schematics," the EI recalled. *"We ran into her later working for that Dario fella. Ten gets you twenty that she delivered it to the AO."*

The ace frowned and vented his rifle. That would explain all the bizarre problems the tech was experiencing and the sudden fluctuations in power. "Can you take us to it, Chief?"

"Partner, it's taking everything I have to make sure we don't fall apart," he responded.

Kaiden looked at the mechanist. "Hey, Genos, do you have any engineer's device on you that can track weird energy signals?"

The Tsuna holstered his hand cannon and took a rectangular device from his pocket. "I have a tri-tool. To be honest, it is only meant to track specific energy readings to help in repairs, but I have modified it. We all have really—"

"Chief, can you at least send him a readout?" he interrupted and the EI nodded and vanished from the HUD.

Genos looked at the monitor of his tool and eyes widened. "Some kind of pulse is creating waves of electric energy and gathering power."

"That doesn't sound good," Kaiden muttered.

The Tsuna shook his head. "It is not. Once it reaches its apex, it will shut down all devices on the island and keep them off even if we destroy it."

Pain continued to wash over his mind, but he dragged in a breath and grasped his rifle tightly. "Which way?"

"To the northeast near the docks." Genos passed him the device.

He nodded. "Guys, follow me!" he shouted to the team. "We have a new target."

Jaxon, Chiyo, and Cameron broke away from the fighting. "Are we not going to the security facility anymore?" the bounty hunter questioned and vented his machine gun.

The ace shook his head. "We'll get there, but we discovered what's causing all of the problems with the tech." As if to prove his point, a group of security bots ran across the plaza a few dozen yards away before they suddenly shut down and fell into one another.

Jaxon looked from the bots to Kaiden. "Where do we need to go?"

"The docks. Genos' tri-tool is tracking it." He held the device up for Jaxon and the others to see.

Chiyo studied the reading quickly. "If we destroy that, all the automated security systems should come online at once. I'm not sure it will be enough to turn this around but it will give everyone remaining a chance to escape."

He nodded but didn't speak as his head continued to throb. Escape? He had begun to realize that maybe that was what they should focus on right now. He wanted to fight until they could push these invaders away, but as he looked into the sky at the massive ship overhead, he wondered if—even if they did escape the island—they could escape that thing.

CHAPTER EIGHTEEN

Sasha took a position at the top of the administration building and aimed his rifle carefully at the enemy forces below. His heart raced as he saw droids throw students and faculty into the crashed pods and seal them inside with shielding.

He placed his fingers against his comm to activate it. "Wolfson...Wolfson, where are you?"

"I've made it into the security facility," his friend responded and swung the edge of his ax into the side of a droid's torso. "I'm heading to the central chamber. I'll get those tunnels open, Sasha."

"Wolfson, they're imprisoning the students," the commander informed him and shifted his aim to the terminal that powered the shielding around the pods. He hesitated and scanned the scene again. The tunnels still weren't open and when he looked at the main gate of the Academy, it was clearly under the enemy's control as dozens of droids stood guard. Some occasionally left the group to pursue students who ran too close to them in search of a way to escape.

He looked at the pod again. Technically, they were safest in there until they could get the tunnels open. If he shorted the terminal and let them escape, would they simply be captured again? Would the bots even bother to leave them alive? The commander cursed quietly. "Wolfson, if you need any kind of clearance or code, let me know and I'll get them to you."

"Do you have Durand with ya?" Wolfson asked and snapped the vent shut on his shotgun.

"I…am the chancellor now," he replied calmly.

The line was quiet for a moment, although he could hear the other man swallow loudly in the mic. "I understand. I'll keep you informed, Sasha. For now, keep yourself safe. I don't know the line of succession but if I'm next, I don't want it."

"Nor did I, my friend." He sighed, adjusted his aim to target a droid below once again, and fired, then followed with several more shots in quick succession. Eight droids were felled in less than six seconds, but the other mechanicals certainly noticed and turned toward the tower. "I won't simply hide but I'll do my best to make sure you don't have to worry." He withdrew from his vantage point but took a moment to look into the sky. Two dropships now headed to the island. "Damn it all, Wolfson. We have more incoming!"

"Droids? I'm sick of them already!" The head officer growled annoyance.

"Dropships instead of pods this time," Sasha informed him, crouched behind another window, and watched the ships land. "We have to move faster, Wolfson. We may have a new problem to deal with." The first vessel hovered over the central plaza and the back ramp opened. A group of soldiers in dark-gray armor and armed with rifles and machine guns leapt from the ship. "But we may also have a chance to spill enemy blood now."

A dozen droids stood waiting outside the ICU of the Nexus' medbay and stared at the barrier that kept them out. Once the others finished their sabotage mission, they would have their way in—or the humans would perish due to their own lack of oxygen.

A small orb rolled beside them. Some looked at it, then back to the shield. They would continue to wait. Gunfire traced the group and all fell after several seconds but didn't react at all. Amber, Flynn, and Marlo ran up. The marksman retrieved the orb as they reached the barrier. "We gotta keep this thing. It's damn handy."

"I hope it has enough juice left," Marlo muttered. "There are hundreds of droids left to deal with."

Amber pulled her tablet out to try to contact her mother to let her know the front was clear, but the device wouldn't activate. "The malfunctions are getting worse." She sighed and banged on the shield. "Doctor Tera Soni! Mom, it's me! Can you hear me?"

"It won't work Amber," Flynn said and placed a hand on her shoulder while Marlo kept watch. "Sound doesn't travel through shields like this."

"Then how do we get their attention?" she asked.

The demolisher tilted his head and gestured at the ceiling with his gun. "Do you think they can see us through this camera?"

His teammates turned their attention to a small, spherical camera overlooking them. Amber walked up to it. "I don't think it's on but it's not damaged."

"It's not likely to simply shut off in an emergency," Flynn reasoned. "Do you think it was deactivated remotely?"

"If it was, it would have been turned off by someone in the administration wing with—shit!" The medic took her sub-machine gun out and raced through the hall. Marlo and Flynn almost tripped over each other to try to catch up.

"They are already there," she shouted over her shoulder as the other two increased their pace. "The droids have control now—the oxygen."

The marksman rushed ahead and nodded briskly as he came up beside her. "We'll save them, Amber. Lead the way."

She nodded and they sprinted to the west side of the medbay and the administration section. While they encountered no droids yet, they began to find certain sections cut off by sealed doors. She was able to redirect them, but her teammates could tell that every delay was getting to her.

Amber pointed at a doorway, this one locked but unsealed. Marlo rushed up and broke it in with two mighty kicks. The door jerked from its hinges and collided with a droid that stood behind it. The mechanical's partners turned to fire at the team. Flynn and Amber ran up behind

Marlo and fired at the enemy while the demolisher drove the butt of his gun against the head of the recovering droid in front of him.

Even with their suppressive fire, something pierced his shoulder and he roared in pain when electricity coursed through him. Amber and Flynn cried out in concern, but the heavy simply gritted his teeth and yanked the spike out. He scowled and looked around to find the droid that had fired it, only to see two of them preparing their next attacks.

In a moment of either instinct or blind rage, he charged the two mechanicals instead of falling back and bulldozed his large body into them. Amber came up and fired at one while he swung his gun repeatedly into the head of the other.

"Hey, hey. I'm damn sure it's down, mate," Flynn said and tried to pull Marlo up from the ground and snap him out of his rage.

It seemed to work. The demolisher took a few long, deep breaths as his teammate helped him to his feet. He glared at the head of the droid, now full of indentions and cracks across the lining, and rubbed the area where he had been shot. "That hurt like hell, man."

"I'm surprised it didn't do real damage." Flynn chuckled and patted him on the chest. "I'm very sure that could have felled a rhino."

Marlo shook his head, his forehead still creased with a trace of anger, but he flashed a smile. "They should have tripled the wattage if they wanted me to lay down." He looked at Amber. "Sorry about that. Where to now?"

She stood and looked at the other end of the hall and

the rooms around them. "It looks like we're in the middle of the administration offices. We either need to find the security station or go below to the maintenance room."

"My guess is that the bots are in the security station. That's where they can hook themselves up to the console and get remote access, right?" the demolisher asked.

"Right, but that's why we should head to the maintenance room," she countered and checked her weapon. "Even if we wipe them out, we don't know if we can take control right now. Whatever is affecting our tech doesn't seem to affect them. Maybe if we destroy them all, the system will simply shut down or lock us out."

"And it'll be different in the maintenance room?" Flynn asked.

"That's where one of the oxygen tanks is," she stated and began to move again. "We can unlock that and manually direct it to the ICU, then we'll take care of the droids."

"We'll save your mom and the others first," Marlo summarized and vented his shotgun. "Then we'll get to the fun part."

"It's clear," Silas called and motioned for the others to follow him out of the engineer's workshop building. The group of students—all wielding modified engineering tools or devices as weapons—made their way out. The battle raged on as students, faculty, and security guards continued to fight the wave of bots. Raul noticed something in the air to his left.

"A dropship," he told the others and pointed at the vessel as it flew away.

Luke watched it leave before he looked in the direction from which it had come. "What did it drop?"

"Look!" One of the engineering students pointed at a trio of armed soldiers wearing gray armor with a white insignia on the chest.

"Who are these guys?" Mack asked and held his gauntlet up.

"That insignia…" Raul muttered, his eyes narrowed and his expression thoughtful. "I think I've seen it before in the Nexus newsletter every now and then. That's the crest of the WC Ark Academy in Russia."

"Do you think they're here to help?" another engineer asked.

"Do you think they could have gotten here that fast if they were?" Silas countered and took a few steps forward as one of the ark students primed their gun.

The rest of the group saw this and spread out as the other invaders took aim. "Put your weapons down and surrender to us," the one in the center shouted. His voice unnerved the enforcer. It sounded unnatural and weirdly gleeful like the warning wasn't a threat or an order but some kind of formality.

"Or you'll attack fellow Ark students?" Luke challenged.

The invaded tilted his head and focused on the titan. "Or we'll kill inferior ones," he stated and his finger squeezed the trigger.

CHAPTER NINETEEN

Silas was not equipped with a helmet of any kind, let alone one with an EI visor that would have allowed him to use his battle suite, slow his perception of time, and quicken his reflexes. And yet, when he saw the light of the blot fired from the gun, he felt as if he watched it discharge slowly and move toward the group. He reacted in kind and yelled for the others to spread out as he shoved one of the engineers to the side before he broke away quickly to avoid the shot himself. It didn't even graze his arm, but the burning heat of plasma was enough to scorch it as it passed overhead. He put it out of his mind and rolled to the side, pushed to his feet, and sprinted around the enemy soldiers. Time resumed its normal course and his breath quickened as he readied his makeshift weapon. He would have to get in close.

The Ark soldiers began to spread out and fire at the Nexus students. One of the engineers tossed Luke his weapon, a robotic arm cannon detached from a model that was installed with a real core. But as the titan caught it out of the air, the engineer was hit and immediately fell. Anger and shock surged in and he spun and pressed the manual switch the engineer had installed in the arm that caused it to charge and fire. Three Ark fighters broke off from their group and avoided the blast. Raul raced across the court, held the rod up, and shouted to the titan, "Luke, switch!"

He nodded, held the gauntlet up as the sides fanned out to make a shield, and ran over to the tracker. Raul caught the cannon and tossed him the electrified rod. He turned to face an invader only several yards away. The man fired and the blast struck the gauntlet, which absorbed it, but the force of the impact knocked him back. A bolt streaked from behind him and forced his adversary to dodge, which gave him an opening. Raul nodded to him and ran off to help the others.

Luke always prided himself on his speed. Heavies weren't exactly known for it, but even without his bounce jets, he was the fastest of them all in his armor. And without it? He reached his attacker faster than the soldier could even believe was possible. The man drew a long blade from a sheath on the back of his armor and thrust forward to stab the titan. Luke simply batted it away, took the rod, and drove it into his opponent's chest as he pressed the trigger. The Ark soldier's armor dulled the shock somewhat but it was effective enough that he couldn't pull the trigger of his gun.

Using the temporary advantage, Luke forced his opponent to the ground and kicked the rifle and blade away before he removed the rod and swung his boot onto the soldier's chest. "You said we're inferior, right?" the titan recalled as he brandished the sparking device in front of the man's visor. "If you're among the best you guys have to offer, you're both inferior and a liar." With that, he raised his boot and stamped it into the soldier's helmet. The blow might have killed him or simply knocked him out, but he needed to help his friends now that he had no distractions.

He took one more look at the beaten soldier and his eyes widened. Through the shattered visor, he saw one eye open to reveal inhumanly pale eyes with some kind of light pulsing through them.

General Nolan watched the battle below and grew steadily more irate. They hadn't made the progress they should have, for one thing, but the other problem was the Ark soldiers. He had given them express orders to subdue the students for reconstruction and only take their lives in extreme circumstances. But it seemed they must have not heard him correctly and seemingly did the opposite. For every student they knocked out or captured, they either killed or maimed two or three others.

"Get Damyen on the comms," he snapped to those around him and strode away from the monitors and to his captain's seat.

"Sir, he may still be in the middle of taking over his next battleship," one of his aides informed him, only to back down when the general glared at him.

"He should be done by now," he stated, and his voice shifted between a growl and hiss. "And if he's not, it would only be another show of his incompetence. He's had all the advantages in his little raids and should be able to catch a two-hundred-crew ship within fifteen minutes of boarding. Get him on the comms."

"Right away, sir!" The aide saluted and ran to his station as Nolan sat and activated a holoscreen.

It didn't take long for the World Council Ark Academy chancellor to answer. He beamed a toothy grin and his long black hair stuck to the side of his face and neck from being trapped in a helmet. "Ah, General! Are you calling to congratulate me on my latest acquisition? I'm surprised, you know. I didn't think I had sent out the—"

"You haven't, Orlov, and I need to talk to you about your students," the general interrupted and leaned forward. "Exactly how well-trained are they, exactly? You followed the protocol in their construction, correct?"

"All the unwilling ones, of course," Damyen stated with a dismissive wave of his hand. "What is this about, Nolan?"

"I gave them express orders that they are defying!" he shouted and thumped the side of his chair. "You tell me, Damyen. Is something wrong with their tuning? Perhaps they feel threatened by the Nexus students?" He tilted his head and waited for a reply from the chancellor.

The man frowned, rolled his shoulders back, and regarded the general warily. "What were your orders?"

"To bring the Nexus students in alive unless they lacked the ability to do so," Nolan retorted. "They've mostly fired lethal rounds and made no attempt to comply. The students are one of the primary reasons we attacked Nexus first."

"Hmm, that and to make a statement," Damyen recalled. "And I see the issue. Well, perhaps not an issue, but they are following my personal order."

"Personal order?" he demanded and stretched the words out in annoyance. "And what would that be?"

"To only spare only those who are worthy," the chancellor said casually. "We do not need the whelps and weaklings. Should you find the boss' treasure, we will want to reconstruct the good ones, ja?"

"That wasn't for you to decide," he countered.

"I believe Merrick will agree with me but I am willing to take the punishment." Damyen studied the general a little arrogantly. "Do you simply want fodder, Nolan? I want an army of humanity's best to show any threats— including our alien 'friends'—what we have to throw against the coming disaster." He smiled as he studied the face of the general, who hadn't given him an answer. "Speaking of which, how goes the retrieval of the device?"

Nolan was silent. He sat upright in his chair and looked at a monitor next to him. "We are still searching for it right now but we will find it."

"Oh? Good, I'm rooting for you. Truly, if you find it, that means more soldiers for me."

His eyes narrowed at the chancellor. "That you are training for me, don't forget that, Damyen."

"Sir! Leda has arrived," Nolan's aide informed him. "She has the device, sir. Should we get it ready?"

The general looked silently at the other man before he turned to address his crew member. "Have it prepared, but the trap we have set will be sufficient. We can use the device once the EI is trapped. It will be more efficient that way. Make sure Leda is ready. Emission transport always makes her a little...aloof once she arrives."

"Yes, sir." The aide saluted once more and rushed away.

He refused to look at Damyen and instead, concentrated on the fight below.

"Damyen, whatever disagreements we may have, we both have orders to follow. I will not use any further soldiers if they will disobey orders. When Merrick asks me why, I will tell him what you've told me and we can see if he truly does agree with you." He took a breath and clenched his teeth for a moment. "Are you willing to see how that turns out?"

"It would be best not to bother," the chancellor retorted before he chuckled quietly. "I'll send you another group and they'll follow your orders to the letter. As for the current batch...there are only a few dozen of them for a trial. How much damage could they do?"

The general scowled at the screen as he watched a soldier blast a door down and be tackled by a group of desperate students. Several other invaders assisted to remove them and prepared to fire.

"Too much damage if this is the best humanity has to offer," he said, mostly to himself as he turned the holo-screen off and ended the communication. He crossed his legs and leaned back. It was taking time for the professor to make his play. Nolan wasn't completely sure how it would come, but he was ready for any number of tactics. Still, he felt confident that the professor would grow desperate and use every advantage he had—including one that would become their advantage with the right cards played.

"Prepare the main cannon, would you?" he ordered a group of soldiers in front of him. "Let's get them properly motivated."

CHAPTER TWENTY

Dario lit a cigar and placed the burner in his pocket as he looked at the multitude of screens in front of him. Paris, Sydney, Beijing, London, Vox, Tokyo, Toronto, and many other major cities were either in the middle of a terrorist attack or a mass malfunction of droids that led to a massacre. Currently—he smiled at the ashes surrounding the room—the WC found itself significantly understaffed.

Although he had to give them some credit. The defense and retaliation they mounted had begun to show dividends. He had been able to push most of the military and security forces down several floors and even out of the building but now, they made slow progress up again. He did, after all, have a finite number of droids at his disposal —but he was about to have a hell of a lot more, he realized when he checked his tablet and saw three dots heading his way that would arrive in a few short minutes. Those should do the trick.

He wasn't under any illusion that this would be enough to stop the WC from functioning indefinitely. Given that they had control of the planet's entire military, they could brute-force their way in soon enough. The AO could probably do some damage to that military might but that would be a bad play for the future. And that was what this was all about, wasn't it?

The assassin pushed himself away from the console and headed to the hangar. Damyen should have made his latest acquisition by now and would begin his tour within a day. The other Ark Academies wouldn't be as well defended as Nexus and their Animus systems would be more malleable for their purposes. All the tests Jensen and Juro had run proved that their current system would be sufficient in those students' reconstruction…with a few casualties, of course.

Still, these were acceptable statistics. That was always the important metric of war.

Another wave of pain swamped Kaiden as he and his team reached a clearing with the main entrance to the docks only a few yards and many droids away.

"Kaiden!" Chiyo gasped as the ace fell to one knee. Genos helped him up as Jaxon and Cameron took point and began to fire and clear a path.

"I'll be fine. We'll be fine, right, Chief?" He looked up to see a slightly faded version of the EI's avatar but he nodded.

"Still, the disruptions are increasing. We need to deal with this thing before everything gets discombobulated and all that junk."

"Not to jinx us, but why are our weapons still functioning?" he asked and glanced at his gun to double-check that it still was.

"Whatever these energy readings are, they are targeting systems. The more complex they are, the easier they are to disrupt. Energy and kinetic weapons are complex in their own right, but no system controls them, at least not the models you have."

The ace swayed a little on his feet and shook his head as he and Chiyo joined Jaxon and Cameron in the fight. "This is one of the few times Wolfson's love of old and archaic things proves helpful."

"Look over there—guards!" the bounty hunter shouted. A group of several security officers was engaged in a fight with bots farther down the harbor. "Do you think they are here for that device too?"

"They could simply be trying to clear the area," Jaxon suggested. "Although it would be a fool's errand with how many are coming from the water."

"Whatever they are here for, we have more firepower with them. Let's help them!" Kaiden led the others toward the heated battle and Genos and Chiyo covered their flank. The bots seemed relentless, but as more students fought back or distracted them, it gave the group enough room to make their way to the officers. Once there, however, they had a little difficulty actually helping as now, all the droids' main threats were grouped together in one position, which made them a tempting target.

"What are you doing here?" one of the guards shouted, vented his machine gun, and drew his pistol to fire with that while his gun cooled.

"We wanted to ask you that," he replied, eliminated a leaping droid, and hastily dodged a spike. "We want to locate the device that's causing all these malfunctions and power drops."

This seemed to get the guard's attention. He vented his pistol while he snapped the one on his machine gun shut and continued to fire. "Where is it?"

"Long story—we're kind of feeling it out." He saw an arrow appear in front of him and point him farther down the wharf. "Down at the warehouses close to the edge of the island."

The man nodded and glanced at his team. "We need that device located and shut down. Try to contact the head officer."

"Wolfson? Did you see him?" Kaiden asked.

"He's the one who sent us here to get the ships ready to help with evacuations," the officer stated. "But getting the thing that's causing all these problems is a priority. We can't get ships in the air or in the water if they don't function."

"That's definitely the right idea," he agreed. "The name is Kaiden Jericho."

"Call me Haldt," the man replied. "Kaiden, huh? Wolfson's mentioned you to some of the other officers and it's gotten back to me. You've impressed him."

"I hoped the pain was worth something." A net was fired at them but the officer drew a blade and sliced it cleanly. "We need to get away from these things. There are too many to stand and fight them."

"And the ones with fresh shields aren't budging." The officer looked down the harbor for a moment. "Come with me. Everyone, form up and keep them at a distance. I have a plan."

The ace nodded. He certainly didn't have one at the moment. The group began to run as one and followed Haldt along the piers. He turned hard right into the warehouses and ran down the trails. Kaiden wondered if he knew where they kept the spare weapons and thought that Sasha or Chiyo might think of him as having tunnel vision right now. The truth, though, was that he didn't see an alternative other than simply shooting more with bigger guns.

The security officer, however, did seem to have an alternative. He found the warehouse he was looking for and began to open the gate while members of his and Kaiden's team kept the droids at bay and dodged their attacks. "Quick, in here."

"What? We'll be literally boxed in," Cameron shouted. He scowled at the attackers and fell back when several darts whistled over his head and thunked into the warehouse walls behind him.

"Trust me. Get in and head to the back." He pointed to two of his teammates. "Kara, Eckles, get your remotes primed."

The two nodded and reached to their belts as they ran into the warehouse. Kaiden was the last to enter and Haldt shut the door behind him. He removed several small, circular devices from his belt.

"I'm fairly sure the door will only hold them for seconds rather than minutes," the ace pointed out with his gun aimed at the door.

"I'm counting on them getting in here," the man replied

as he activated the disks and began to place them on boxes and barrels. "Get to the back. There is another exit."

He nodded and didn't hesitate despite his confusion. Kara and Eckles placed their small circles on other items around the warehouse and he realized they were mines. When he saw what they were sticking to, he smiled.

The door in the front began to give way under the assault as one of the other officers ushered him out of the back door. The three inside hurried through behind them before Haldt shut the door and Kara and Eckles retrieved their detonators.

Haldt held his up as the entire group ran and called out a countdown from five. When he reached zero, the three pressed their switches and the warehouse behind them erupted in a massive explosion that engulfed the buildings around it in mushrooming flame. Kaiden looked back but turned away quickly and began to run faster when he saw debris begin to plummet from above. The warehouse had been filled with chemical runoff and explosive material from the tech and engineering departments that had yet to be properly disposed of.

It wasn't an entirely acceptable way to dispose of it, but he decided he wouldn't bring that up.

"Well, that should give us a little time to breathe," Haldt said and looked at Kaiden over his shoulder. "Can you lead the way?"

"I'm on it," he affirmed. Another dull ache throbbed in his head but he shook it off and pushed forward. The sooner they were rid of this thing, the better they would all be.

CHAPTER TWENTY-ONE

"Is there anything you can give us before we head in, Chief?" Kaiden asked as he, Haldt, and the rest of the team approached the location of the disruptor.

"H-honestly, I'm only tryin' to...k-k-ke-eep it together," the EI admitted. *"Detecting...e-en-nergy readings i-inside. There are droids...ob-obviously."*

"Obviously," Kaiden repeated, checked his gun, and wiped his brow. When a hand settled on his shoulder, he looked behind him at Chiyo, whose face displayed real concern. He gave her a swift nod and assured her silently that he would be fine. He would be even better when they were through, of course.

"My g-g-guess is...ex-expect heavy resi-s-stance." Chief's stuttering seemed worse.

"No other signals?" Kaiden inquired.

"No. C-counting the ones we've d-d-de-ealt with so f-far, though, I-I read a c-couple of high-higher output e-e-energy readings that c-c-could mean ma-m-malfunctioning droids or different m-models."

141

The ace frowned and glanced at Haldt, who was on the other side of the doors. The officer held his weapon up and nodded and he returned the gesture.

"Be on your guard. We don't wanna deal with any more surprises today," the security officer ordered.

"We might actually have one. My EI is saying there are potentially a couple of bigger bots in there," he warned.

The man nodded. "Mine said the same thing. I'm sure there are more than only a couple in there, given how critical this thing is to disrupting our equipment. It'll be heavily guarded."

"It's not a big deal. We only gotta blow this thing up," Cameron interjected. "Back at Ramses, we had to keep it intact. This'll be way easier."

"Do you know what this thing is?" one of the officers asked.

Kaiden shrugged. "We have a general idea. It gives me the same feeling that another device did on a previous gig."

"I don't feel anything," Eckles commented.

He sighed and shook his head. "That's a long story so let's wrap this up. I'd like to destroy this device sooner rather than later."

"I might be able to disassemble it for later uses, perhaps," Genos suggested and checked his belt. "I think I was able to grab—"

"Too late, I have dibs!" Kaiden, assisted by Haldt, kicked the door and a loud clang echoed in the warehouse as it fell. The two entered with their weapons ready but there was no need for any kind of search. Directly ahead in the center of the room stood a pyramid-like device guarded by heavy shielding, but tears were visible in the barrier. He assumed it must be succumbing to the device's own effect. Two droids immediately stepped in front of their target. Larger than the other Arbiter bots, they boasted heavier armor and sharp blue eyes that stared at the group. Each had a cannon for an arm with the second arm free, although one of them drew it back and cast it forward and a long blade emerged from the top.

"It looks like those are the bigger energy readings," Haldt muttered. He scowled at the glowing lights above as several other droids stalked across the frames and suspended walkways.

"Target located, Kaiden Jericho," the blade-wielding bot stated and stepped forward.

"Who did you piss off?" Eckles asked as he and two other guards moved to the front.

"Oh, too many people," Kaiden admitted. "It's kind of nice to be known, really."

"Are you gonna blush?" Cameron asked.

"K-Kaiden...above y-you," Chief shouted.

He jumped to the side instinctually as a droid fell and its blades dug into the floor. Jaxon shot it before it could tear itself free and the group scattered as the enemy began to fire.

Beams, spikes, darts, and kinetic rounds erupted from all sides. One of the guards tossed a shield emitter to Genos, who caught and activated it, then thrust it into the ground as a dome formed around the team. Kaiden, however, broke out when he saw that the larger droids were far more interested in him than anyone else. He unhooked a thermal from his belt. There was no impetus to spare the device this time, and the fact that the droids seemed to be charging their cannons meant they didn't seem interested in keeping him alive like the others.

When he activated the grenade and threw it at them, however, one of them fired at it. The grenade was caught in a purple energy field and exploded but didn't damage the barrier. It was some kind of containment field, so he had to assume that they did want him alive. That gave him even more reason to destroy them.

Jaxon ran out of the safety of the shield armed with a shock grenade. He tossed it so that it skipped along the ground and beneath the droid's positions. It detonated and electricity engulfed the mechanicals, but they seemed undamaged. The electricity faded and hadn't even been able to successfully damage the disruptor.

They must have had conduction mods, but the Tsuna ace couldn't think about that for long as one of the bots turned and fired at him. He fell prone and the shot rocketed overhead and amusingly, caught one of the other Arbiter bots in the containment field behind him. Jaxon flipped over and fired, but his blasts bounced off the droids' shielding. They would need something with more power.

"Firing ballistic rounds," Kara shouted as she and Eckles raced out from behind the shield and fired several rounds apiece at the enemy. The ballistics struck the shields, exploded, and finally forced the droids back. Jaxon pushed to his feet and focused his attention on eliminating the remaining mechanicals. He finally felt a sense of accomplishment after he'd dealt with what seemed like an unending horde of them. Relieved, he realized that there was only a handful left in there, although they had to hurry before more arrived.

"Lethal force required. Changing to beam." A whir and hiss issued from the droids. Kaiden destroyed an Arbiter bot and turned to look at the larger mechanicals and his eyes widened. "Get down!" he bellowed.

The guards scattered as the enemy fired. Powerful beams streaked from their cannons and battered their shield. The power of the two together shattered it almost instantly and they surged forward to attack the guards. One security officer was able to avoid them but an Arbiter bot took the opportunity to fall from the roof above. It impacted with the man's chest, drew an arm back, and hammered a metal fist into his helmet. Blood coated its hand when it removed it.

The droids ceased their fire and several vents opened on their cannons. The second droid drew its blade as well and they both began to stalk their prey. The ace found a moment of peace behind a pillar and checked his remaining thermals. He had five left and wondered if he should simply charge them all and detonate them near the disruptor. The shield, however, was still in place.

"Chief, how sturdy is that shield?" he asked.

"Losing stability rapidly... Emitter...almost finished charging," the EI responded and his voice cut in and out. Kaiden could feel the stress in his mind, but he kept it at bay. They had to hurry and end this, but he couldn't risk losing all his thermals if they would simply be nullified by the shield. He needed to have that shield broken or drained. "Genos!"

"Yes, Kaiden?" the Tsuna called to him as he continued

to fire at the approaching droids and dodged another spike.

"Your nanos—throw them!" he ordered.

"Where? At the droids?" Genos asked.

"At the device—all of them. Do it!" he yelled, held the trigger on the thermal container down, and sprinted forward.

His teammate retrieved the three nano grenades he had. He was worried that with the disruptions, they would not prove very useful, but if Kaiden needed them, he would use them. He backed away and inched closer to the device as he saw the vents shut on the droids' cannons. Quickly, he activated the three grenades and lobbed them toward the disruptor. One of the droids saw them and turned to fire but was interrupted by Kara's ballistic shots from across the warehouse. The mechanical snapped to face her position and fired. She cried out in pain at the same moment that the nanos exploded out of their container.

Ripples traced along the shielding almost as soon as the grenades detonated. Nanos were attracted to the closest source of energy when they didn't have a directive. While he didn't like to simply hope things would work out considering the circumstances, this was the best option if it worked correctly. It looked like it did as what remained of the shield began to thin and disintegrate. But the device itself began to glow brighter. He could almost see the energy pulse off it as it prepared to erupt. Hastily, he removed his finger from the thermal container's trigger and hurled it at the base of the device. It knocked against the side before it exploded. A massive blast rocked the warehouse. He and others were hurled into the walls or pillars by the force of it.

Kaiden, far more used to this than he ought to be, was able to recover fairly quickly and held his rifle at the ready. "Chief, are you good?" he asked and almost felt lighter in some way.

"Attention. Nexus Academy is under attack. Defensive systems are activating. All students should make their way..."

"That's the security alert!" Cameron shouted, relief evident in his voice although he was quickly reminded of the immediate threat when he heard the hum of a droid's cannon. He turned to the glow of the weapon and the robot's eyes amongst the dust and smoke. Before he could respond, several explosions behind the enemy's back toppled it. Haldt stood calmly and added more ballistic rounds to his weapon.

"We still have more droids to deal with," he stated and gestured to where the other big mechanical shook off the debris that had fallen on it from the explosion. Kaiden fired at it, as did Jaxon and Chiyo. One by one, all the remaining soldiers targeted it in a concerted barrage that destroyed first its shields and then it before it could fire. Unfortunately, they did not finish it before it could retaliate.

When the droid fell, it began to glow and Chief showed Kaiden a reading that its temperature was rising rapidly. "It's going to blow!"

"Everyone, get moving!" Haldt ordered and the group sprinted out of the warehouse and away from the droid attempt to destroy the team.

Once outside, they were able to see turrets come online

and the defensive barriers activate all along the island. The ace felt a sense of excitement and hope now. But when he looked into the sky, it was dashed almost as quickly by the sight of the titanic ship above charging its main cannon, which was aimed at the center of the island.

CHAPTER TWENTY-TWO

"Professor! It's working."

"What is?" Laurie had his answer before the technician could respond. When his personal interface reappeared and his console booted up, he wasted no time. "Get the defense array online immediately and all the hatches open if Wolfson has not done so already. Bring the network up and contact every student and faculty member you can. We need to get them to safety."

"Right away, sir."

The professor opened a holoscreen. "Cyra, are you there?"

"I am. It's good to hear from you, Professor!" she responded, her smile wide despite the fatigue in her eyes. "Were you able to locate the source of the disruptions?"

"Actually, no. We've worked on it but all our—"

"Laurie! I'm finally able to get through to ya," Wolfson said cheerfully as he appeared on another screen. "Everything is back online. The tunnels should open now and the security bots are reactivating. Good work!"

"It wasn't me, Wolfson," he admitted. "I've been blind since the start of this. We weren't able to get a lock on whatever caused the problem."

"Really? Then who— Hold a moment Laurie." The head officer looked to the side. "Yes, Haldt? Were you able to— Eh? Took care of the disruption? Where was— Kaiden!"

"Kaiden?" Laurie would have laughed if it weren't for the chaos surrounding him at the moment. Even when he had no idea what he was doing, the ace always seemed to find a way to be useful.

"The ship's cannon is coming online!" That caught his attention instantly. He looked at a camera feed from the main plaza and craned it up at a definitive glow in the ship's cannon.

"Sir, from what we're able to discern about the ship's model, that cannon is currently at thirty percent of a charge," one of the technicians explained hastily.

"We have control again. Everything is working and we will execute the plan," he stated. "Prepare the array and target the ship."

"Right away." A trio of technicians rushed over to the array to help the others already working on it.

"Some of the systems are still rebooting. We'll have it ready in approximately three minutes, Professor."

Laurie nodded and took a position at the main console as Cyra's monitor appeared next to him and Wolfson signed off. "When we're in, we'll have access to the ship's EI. We'll cut the power to everything but the main engine. If they do not surrender, we'll threaten to send them into the ocean and overheat the core."

She looked at him in surprise "A blast like that, Professor—I mean, the ship is massive!"

"I said threaten, Cyra. There's no need to actually do so," he pointed out. "It would be a waste. How are you holding up down there?"

"Much better now that all the defenses are activating," she stated. "We had to be selective on what we powered up and had people running spare generators and using older model power cores for the bots. Everything is working as intended now."

"Very good. Keep it up. We've weathered the storm now." He wanted to believe his words more than he did, but he couldn't shake a feeling of foreboding that overtook him and decided he shouldn't get cocky. "We'll end this soon."

"The array is ready, sir. We're connecting it to the enemy ship's EI," Gustav reported. The professor watched intently as the connection was established. It didn't matter what kind of security defended the EI. The array would connect to it directly and focus on the code that either his father or Laurie himself had created.

Their opponents either knew this or expected they would find a workaround. Once the connection was established, he was greeted by a stream of constantly changing code that included orders and directions that couldn't possibly be followed by a ship's EI rapidly appear and disappear from view.

"What's going on?" one of the techs asked. "Is something wrong with the connection? The system?"

Laurie bit his lip in frustration. "No, nothing of the sort," he snapped. "They've cracked the EI—several EIs—

and created redundant ones that are issued junk orders or commands. They are cycled through every few seconds. Only one is given the real commands at any moment." He let his head hang as he slumped against the console and laughed. "Honestly, I've heard of hackers doing something similar to defend their own consoles or systems but nothing on a scale this large. Ship EIs are incredibly complex on their own and there are significant risks if you make this your defense."

"Can we... Can you do anything about it, sir?" Gustav asked.

The professor dragged in a deep breath as he examined the console once again. "It's changing too fast...the cycling... I can't keep up with it enough to even form a plan. By the time I issue a command, the main EI will have switched."

"*I can take over, Professor,*" Aurora suggested, her voice soothing.

He took his EI pad out and placed it against the console. "Even with the quick cycling, Aurora has sufficient power and will be able to comb through the junk code quite easily." Still, he hesitated. If they discovered her inside their systems, they would have time to purge her, but she should be able to escape even quicker than they could catch her. Finally, he nodded, took a cord from the EI pad, and connected it to the console. "Be quick, Aurora. Simply disable the ship and freeze the cycling for easier control, understand?"

"*Of course, Professor.*" Laurie uploaded her into the relay and granted her control of the machine as he stepped away. He watched the constantly changing figures on the screen begin to slow and some of the lights on the ship began to flicker and disappear. She was getting in.

But it was the cannon that he and the others focused on. He glanced at the report—sixty-seven percent and rising. He'd received no alerts yet so Aurora was still in the clear for now.

The monitor froze and the code locked in place. His gaze darted between the monitor, the readouts, and the feed to the ship. Tentatively, he walked forward and whispered. "Aurora?" He almost held his breath while he waited for an answer

There was no reply, although the figures on the screen began to change once more. Laurie stepped back and focused on the readouts. Sixty-seven percent still...sixty-six...it was falling!

The professor looked at the feed as the ship began to darken and the technicians began to smile, checked their monitors, and looked for changes. "The enemy droids are still moving, sir, but the energy readings from the ship are dropping sharply."

"*I apologize for being so quiet, Professor,*" Aurora said and appeared onscreen once again. "*It was more of an effort to freeze the cycling than I had anticipated.*"

He felt relief and placed his hand on the monitor. "It's all right, Aurora. You've done well. Do we have control of the ship?"

"*I will have control in app...appro...stand-by...issu...*" Her avatar flickered, faded, and suddenly vanished. The monitor of the array brightened before it powered down and there was nothing but silence.

JOSHUA ANDERLE & MICHAEL ANDERLE

"Aurora!" he yelled and checked the pad. He had no signal.

"Professor, we're being hailed, by the ship," Gustav informed him.

The professor turned to look at the main screen, which displayed a man with slicked-back gray hair and sharp, dark eyes that bored into him in open scrutiny. "So, Professor Laurie, I wonder if you will be more civil than your chancellor was."

He walked closer to the screen and observed the man he believed to be the leader of this invasion. "You are a member of the Arbiter Organization, aren't you?"

A prideful grin appeared on the man's face and he stood a little straighter. "I am indeed. I am General Nolan Pocock, leader of our military division."

"Pocock?" he muttered quietly. It sounded familiar. "What is it that you want? Why have you attacked our Academy? You should know that this will lead to retaliation from the World Council."

"Eventually, I'm sure," the man retorted. "We will be ready by then, and the council has to deal with their own mess so don't expect their assistance anytime soon."

He didn't bother to respond to the general's statement but he could tell that he wasn't lying or at least believed that the WC was too distracted to come to their aid anytime soon.

"I should congratulate you on what you have been able to accomplish so far. Destroying our disruptor, holding off our attacks...you've even managed to disable parts of my ship." Nolan looked at a tablet or some kind of device. Laurie had to guess as his face was lit up with artificial light. "That last part is most impressive, truly. We expected some kind of attack on the ship and planned for multiple tactics. Most of them had you playing a part, and I'm so glad you did. But even with that preparation, I didn't expect you to do so much damage in such a short window of opportunity."

"Where is Aurora?" he demanded.

"Aurora? Is that the EI's name? Lana will want to know that. She is with us, Professor. You took our EI, so it's only fair that we replace them with yours. And I must say, we're quite grateful. She looks to be even better than anything we could have devised."

"She is my EI and is among the greatest of my creations and all EIs. She can't be cracked or reconfigured to listen to you," Laurie roared, his fists clenched.

"Aurora herself, most likely not," Nolan conceded but his grin returned. "Of course, we only need her system and her power. The EI as a construct is not that important, really. And that we can have."

"What are you talking about?" he asked but the man ignored him.

"I congratulate you for what you've accomplished. But know that you have not won. If anything, this is a small intermission, I would say." The general fixed him with a hard look. "When we resume, I can promise that the second act will be a tragedy. Of course, you can prevent it by persuading all the others down there with you in that Academy to surrender. What do you—"

"That will not happen!" Laurie declared. "And I'm sure Chancellor Durand said the same thing. You may destroy this Academy, but you will not take it."

Nolan frowned, sat in his chair, and crossed his legs. "Not exactly the same but close enough." He breathed deeply and shook his head. "Your courage is admirable but my patience is running thin," he said and glowered to make his point. "We have no desire to destroy our Academy. We have a mission for humanity as a whole, and your students will play an important part although you may not." He finished his statement and the screen shut off. Laurie's lab fell into silence as the professor let his words sink in.

CHAPTER TWENTY-THREE

"Is that the last of them?" Marlo asked and booted the shattered arm of one of the Arbiter bots across the floor.

"For now, it looks like it," Flynn confirmed and rested his rifle against his shoulder. "More can always come but the doctors and patients are what matters right now. How's it looking, Amber?"

"Pix was able to get in. My credentials are still good so they haven't locked us out yet," she informed them as she watched her EI reactivate all the airway systems. "It looks like the power is coming back on too."

"Good timing. Do you think you can make a connection with your mom?" Marlo asked. He set his cannon down for a moment to give him time to stretch his arms.

"I'm trying to get through now, but I haven't had any luck. I think her link is either destroyed or she turned it off to be safe from any potential hacking."

"Or propaganda," the marksman added. "Did you hear what some of those bots spewed out there?"

"It was kinda hard to over all the yelling and gunfire," the demolisher said and ran a hand under his chin. "But I heard them talking about something—laying down our arms or something like that?"

"They were acting so civil about it," Flynn muttered and rolled his eyes. He walked over and knelt beside Amber. "Should we head back to the barrier?"

She took a moment to think and eventually nodded. "Pix can handle the rest but let me grab one thing. The list of sign-ins will show who else is in there and who I can contact."

"All right. Marlo and I will scout ahead." He looked at his large teammate, who nodded and picked his cannon up. The two walked out to make sure their path remained clear while Amber hurried to find the list. She took a moment to look at the room her mother and the others were bunkered in and saw a few dozen green dots. At least they were safe, but she wondered if they should risk taking them out of the relative safety of the ICU and into the battlefield.

Genos looked at the hoverboard on the wall, took it down, and flipped the activation switch. He grinned as it began to hum and the lights glowed. "I believe I can make use of this."

Kaiden, who leaned against the wall of the confiscation office, looked at him and chuckled. "I'm happy for you, buddy." He turned to Officer Haldt as the man entered the office. "So, you get in touch with Wolfson?"

"Yeah. He thanked us for breaking orders. Now that's a

weird feeling," he admitted. "He also asked why you didn't try to call him yourself."

"Chief can't make calls yet. He is still putting everything back together. Taking so many of those pulses has kinda messed with him— Say are my eyes crooked?"

The security officer shook his head. "No. I hope that means something good?"

"I'm worried something might have happened to me too and he's not saying anything," he admitted.

"Guys, I'm getting strong energy readings heading toward the island," Chiyo announced and looked up from her holoscreen.

Kaiden, Haldt, and many of the others walked over to have a look. "More of those super bots we fought?" one of the officers asked.

"No, although there are similar readings closer to the main gate. These are a little different. There are fewer spikes in energy with a more consistent but larger output than the normal bots."

"Which would mean what, exactly?" the ace asked.

Genos took an engineer's gauntlet from one of the boxes and studied the mods as he considered Chiyo's description. "Friend Chiyo, would the color of that reading bleed into blue?"

"It does." She nodded and the entire group focused on him.

He nodded and pulled the gauntlet on. "Then, if I had to make a guess, I would say mechs."

Everyone went quiet and some looked at each other as Genos turned. "Ah, that's not good, is it?"

"Do I need to tell you that they are not ours?" Kaiden

asked. Several loud pounding sounds were audible from outside.

"There are at least five coming in from the harbor and close to our position," Chiyo stated.

"Where is this warehouse filled with ships you need to get to?" Cameron asked.

"And how badly do we need them, exactly?" the ace added.

"All the ships we had prepped on the surface were destroyed during the initial attack." Haldt sighed. "We should still have sufficient numbers in the main port. Those are all shuttles and water carriers so it would make rescue and evacuation much faster." He scrolled across the map and pointed to a building that was about three hundred yards from where they were. "There's a stairwell that will take us down to the hangar, but we'll have to cut through here."

"Where those mechs just showed up." Eckles sighed.

"The tunnels are open now, correct?" Jaxon asked. "Do you think we'll still need to use the shuttles?"

"The emergency tunnels and runways off the island are active now, but how many students will be able to get there while dodging the bots?" Haldt asked. "Not to mention that the tunnels would be useless if the mechanicals simply pursued. They have internal defenses but once they are compromised, the entrance hatches will seal and the pathway will lock down and erupt in a crisis like this. Hopefully, a good number of students will escape but it won't be all of them."

Kaiden placed a hand on the officer's shoulder and nodded. "You don't need to say anything more." The loud sounds from outside now included cannon fire. "Although I would like to hear some opinions on how we can eliminate those things."

"I'm trying to see if I can hack in, but it looks like I can't access their system. Kaitō, what's wrong?"

"It seems the mechs are controlled by cracked EIs, madame," Kaitō informed her. *"That is probably why they weren't a part of the initial invasion group. They don't seem to have the same shielding that the normal droids do. That disruption emitter would have wreaked as much havoc on them as it did on our machines."*

"What? They simply chilled in the lake in case the device was destroyed?" Cameron asked. "Dammit, man, that's a kick in the teeth."

"My guess is that they hoped the loss of our tech would finally push us into surrendering. They do seem to want to take us alive, for the most part," Jaxon interjected. "Now that it's destroyed and that's not an option, they have gone with a more forceful tactic."

"Like hell it's going to work." Kaiden sneered. "All right, we've restocked what we could and found some new toys. But we'll have to think of a way to get through those—"

"I shall take care of them," Genos said. The others looked over as the Tsuna dropped the hoverboard onto the floor and opened the front door. "I shall try to be quick." Before anyone could call out to him, he raced away.

The group sat there for a moment in shock and silence. Kaiden broke that silence when he looked at Jaxon and said, "Let's go and get your suicidal kin, yeah?"

CHAPTER TWENTY-FOUR

Genos whipped around the harbor in search of his targets. He needed to get to the middle of the field and cause an obvious distraction. It had to be something to draw the attention of the enemies in the field so they would focus on him as a primary target and pursue him long enough that his teammates could make it across.

He looked to the east and located his prey. A trio of mechs emerged from the water. They had begun to boot up and their shields weren't online yet so they were vulnerable enough for him to do what he needed to do.

With his gauntlet activated, he adjusted the hand into a clamp as he raced toward them and snatched a droid up along the way. It was a simple Fighter droid with a skinny frame and lightly armored with a basic laser rifle. The mechanical's head spun as if it couldn't comprehend the situation and he crushed its chest in his grasp. He kept the head and swerved around the mechs to get behind them as they began to stand and arm their systems.

The Tsuna lunged off his board and onto the back of

the mech in the middle. He scrambled to the top, tore quickly into the outer metal, and revealed a panel within.

Once he'd exposed the panel, he opened a small port on the head of the robot he had taken. He deactivated his gauntlet, straightened his index finger to release a small set of prongs, and snagged a small cord from inside the panel of the mech. Carefully, the cord clutched in his hand, he placed the robot's head onto the mech and slid the end of the cord into a slot in the port of the head.

The mechs on either side began to turn toward him and he heard the whirring of mechanics working in tandem. The claw of the mech on his left began to fidget and he knew he was cutting it close.

"Genos, what the hell are you doing?" Kaiden demanded over the comms.

"Ah, friend Kaiden, it's good to hear your comms are working now." The mech swung but he held firm. "Just a moment, if you would. It is quite stressful at this time." He peered into the mech's panel again and withdrew some wires.

"No shit! You'll get yourself killed," the ace snapped.

Jaxon joined the conversation. "Where are you, kin? We will assist."

He uncurled his pointer and middle finger and blades emerged on the inside of them to create scissors. Deftly, he snipped a few of the wires and deactivated them. "I'm much obliged, but you are on foot and are vulnerable to the droids. I ask that you look after yourselves while I work on this." He drew his access pistol and shot the device into the back of the droid's head. The huge mechanical on the left began to reach up to grab him and he dropped onto the mech's back. The attacking claw missed and he pulled himself up again and opened the screen on his tablet. He heard energy charging and looked at the mech on his right. It stepped back and turned toward him to aim its cannon.

"Genos, I don't know what the hell you are doing, but you need to—"

"I've borrowed a strategy of yours, Kaiden, and I'm simply adding my skills to it," Genos replied and pressed a button on the gauntlet screen.

The mech he was on raised both its arms to either side. It had a cannon on each arm and they quickly began to charge. Both its comrades moved back once they realized what was going on but it was too late. The cannons fired into the two cockpits and the metal bodies teetered for a moment before they fell.

"What did you do?" Kaiden asked, astonished.

"I'll fill you in later. For now, I need to finish my plan," the mechanist informed him. "Kaiden, you are close, correct?"

"We're closing in—only about fifty yards away."

Genos looked in their direction. "That should be close enough. Please ask the officer with the cannon to be ready to fire when you turn the corner."

He climbed on top of the mech once again and over to the cockpit. Several punches with his gauntlet cracked the shielding and he could see the glowing core within. Above it, a small screen with a moving eye indicated the jockey EI controlling the mech. Not for much longer, of course.

Kaiden and the group ran out of one of the alleys and the officer with the cannon looked inquiringly at him. "That should be enough. Please fire," the mechanist ordered, pushed himself back to the top of the mech, and braced against it.

The Tsuna moved his head to the side when an orb of red light careened into the cockpit. It was followed by a scream and a burning smell. When he looked again, the window had shattered and partially melted and the jockey EI was no longer an issue

"Much obliged," he said in thanks to the ace and officer. Working quickly, he ripped the panel out, caught a few of the wires, and connected them into the core. He then climbed inside and made sure to peer out onto the field for a moment to see if there was any immediate danger. Finally, he reached under the control board and pried it loose.

With a broad grin, he looked around to determine what he had to work with. "Yes. Oh, yes, this will do."

"What is he doing?" Kaiden muttered. "He said he would create a distraction, not take out a few mechs for giggles."

"He is holding his composure incredibly well," Chiyo pointed out.

"And while I would usually appreciate that, I'm worried it will be for nothing if he gets himself killed." His anxiety refused to abate.

Jaxon looked at the downed mechs for a moment and could barely see Genos in the center of the last one standing. He would occasionally poke his head up but he seemed mostly preoccupied with something inside. "Do what he normally says when you run off to do something."

"What would that be? Stand by for a wave of hostiles?" Kaiden snickered.

"Trust him. He will make it work," the Tsuna ace replied.

He looked at him in silence, then focused on the mechs and sighed as he took the cannon off his shoulder and held it in both hands "If he's not done in a few minutes, I'll pull him out of there."

"I don't believe he'll take that long. He works almost as fast as I do," Chiyo assured him.

"Friends, I'm ready. Prepare to run toward our destination," Genos ordered on the comms.

"Gotcha," the ace acknowledged and stretched his legs. "Do you wanna fill us in now or is that still a rain-check?"

"There doesn't appear to be rain during this time. Do not worry, the weather does not affect whether or not I give you information."

"Considering the circumstances, I'll let it slide." He chuckled and spun to obliterate another droid while he waited for the command to sprint.

"Distraction happening in ten seconds."

Genos hopped out of the mech. The boosters on the back began to rotate and its cannons pointed forward and began to charge. The Tsuna veered away on his hoverboard toward the building as the mechanical surged forward. The small droid's head was still attached to it and waved in the wind as the mech surged into a wild run. It began to fire its cannons indiscriminately and destroyed Arbiter droids along its path. A couple of other mechs turned to it and fired. One of its cannons was blown off but the rogue continued to speed forward and fire with its remaining weapon. Other droids began to focus on the rampaging mech as it continued its onslaught. A leg was blown off but the boosters continued to power it over the field.

"That is certainly one way to get all the attention." Kaiden whistled.

"Let's go, Kaiden," Chiyo demanded and leaned forward before she sprinted across the field.

He followed quickly with the cannon held against his chest so he could focus on the goal rather than be tempted to fire at anything.

The mech was finally stopped by another cannon shot. It fell and was approached slowly and cautiously by a few droids. A rapid beeping began and a red light flashed in the damaged torso. The droids turned to flee but the mech self-destructed before they could escape and obliterated them. Two mechs that emerged from the water were hurled back into the lake by the force of the blast.

Genos looked back with a satisfied smile as he coasted toward the dock building with a trail of broken parts, debris, and fire behind him.

CHAPTER TWENTY-FIVE

"Dr. Calloway, are you there?" Amber asked. She was almost halfway down the list when the trio approached the medbay barrier once again. Flynn could hear the battle still raging outside but nothing sounded like it came from within other than their own hurried footsteps. That actually concerned him more.

"Who is this?" a voice replied. "If this is security, I am Dr. Calloway and we are currently—"

"Doctor, it's Amber Soni!" she interrupted and both relief and happiness manifested in her tone. "We're almost outside the barrier, the power is back on, and we've eliminated all the bots we've seen along the way. We can guide you to the exit."

"Amber! One moment, let me give the comm to your mother." Rustling followed as the doctor transferred the device to Dr Soni, but once she was on, her mother's own momentary joy was evident.

"Amber, I'm so glad you're okay," she began. "What does it look like now? There was so much commotion when those machines arrived. We grabbed everyone we could but the evacuation paths were locked—"

"I know, Mom. For now, it appears to be safe," the battle medic said as she and her teammates finally rounded the corner into the ICU hallway. "Mom, we're outside the barrier and can escort you and the others out."

"If the power is back, maybe the tunnels are open again," Marlo suggested. "It would be better than trying to escort them across the island."

"That's a good point," Flynn agreed and placed a hand on Amber's shoulder. "Ask her where the nearest exit is."

"I know where it is. It's basic safety meeting stuff and you have to listen to the speech even if you're only a volunteer," she responded. "Is anyone seriously injured in there?"

Dr. Soni was quiet for a moment. "We lost some of the injured. The droids took some but killed most of the faculty. Even with the instruments and medical supplies we have available in here, we weren't able to help them."

She nodded solemnly and took a deep breath. "I'm sorry, Mom. I know that's hard. But we need to focus on the ones we can save right now. Is everyone else all right?"

"Yes. Everyone else is conscious and able to move on their own. We can leave if you are ready," the doctor replied. Amber looked at Marlo and Flynn who nodded to her as each held their weapons up.

"Go ahead and disengage the barrier and we'll get out of here." She backed away from the door and waited for the medbay staff and patients inside to exit.

Five Ark troops stood outside the entrance to the medbay building. "Do we really have to bother with this one?" one asked. "It looks like the droids took care of most of it."

"And almost all the droids inside have been destroyed. Something is obviously still kicking in there," another retorted. "This should be a quick clean-up."

"That's my point. This is not a true battle with the Nexus students. Most aren't even armed," the first one protested. "I wanted to earn my stripes but I feel like a glorified janitor right now."

"Quit your whining. We have a job to finish," his teammate reminded him and took a step forward before a hand on his shoulder stopped him.

He looked back and tilted his head. The soldier who had stopped him held a finger up. "Remember, we are looking for others to join our army."

He shrugged his shoulder free but nodded. "I know, but I've yet to see any who are worthy."

"What do we do now, sir?" one of the security team asked as they made their way to the surface.

"You and the bots will make sure those tunnels and paths are clear for the students and get the evacuation started in earnest," Wolfson ordered. "I need to get to the armory."

"The armory, sir?" the guard asked. "I thought you said we are evacuating."

"We are," he confirmed. "Which means we'll leave the island in the hands of these bastards. I intend to hobble them as much as I can while I'm still here. While Haldt and

Kaiden get the ships ready, I'll prepare as many weapons as I can to ship out. Then, I'll rig the rest to explode when these bastards get close."

"Are you sure you don't need any help, sir?"

The head officer studied a map of the Academy on his tablet. "The students and teachers need help more than I do. And there are other security members on the way. I can assist them, and they can then assist me." He shoved the tablet against her chest. "You're in charge of any of the forces still here in the facility. All of you get out there and make me proud."

"Yes, sir!" The guard saluted and ran off. Wolfson went left down the hall to his office. He needed to stock up and he should still have his small stash waiting in the locker for him. When he entered his office, a light flashed over him as a turret scanned him. It recognized him and retracted into the ceiling. Despite all the digs he took at Laurie, seeing the defenses working in a time of crisis was oddly calming.

He placed his shotgun on the table, walked to his locker, and quickly punched the code in. As the door unlocked, something hummed behind him. He spun quickly as a heated blade lashed at him, knocked it aside with his gauntlet, and kicked out. The kick missed when a figure in dark armor flipped back, landed on his desk, and picked his shotgun up. "Baioh Wolfson," she said, her voice low and oddly monotone as she took aim. "Target acquired and eliminated."

When she fired, she expected a blast of laser fire to melt through his armor and kill him instantly. Instead, only a few ember-like flashes puffed out as the weapon made a hissing noise. The kick, however, was still there, one powerful even for him to handle. The featherweight assassin was hurled off the table and she catapulted into the hallway.

Wolfson chuckled as he approached and brandished his hand cannon. He shoved his boot into her chest while she was on the floor. "Why do you flippy assassin types always think heavies are an easy kill? Because we can't move fast?" He lowered his weapon until it was aimed at her head. "It doesn't mean much in such a small room, and you should have taken a look at that shotgun. Do you think I would have put it down if it was functional? The core has given out after all the rapid venting."

The woman made no response, which distracted him a little. Had she knocked herself unconscious on impact? She had a helmet on so that was unlikely. He stooped, reached under the helmet, and unclasped the locks so he could pull it off. What he was greeted with was blank eyes, dark spots dotted around her temple, and glowing lines under her skin.

At first, these horrific marks made him believe she was a golem. But there was too much detail in her features and she had hair, not the normal indicators of a golem. If she were really human, what had they done to her?

"Captain Wolfson!" an officer's voice called over the comms and gunfire chattered in the background.

"What's wrong?" he asked.

"The droids have made another push against the main gate of the security building. There are now armored troops with them as well."

"Yeah, I met one." He hurried to the locker, removed one of the damaged gauntlets on his armor, and replaced it with a new, mismatched black one with spiked rods that protruded around the knuckles. A memory surfaced and he smiled but hastily pushed it aside. He then selected a container of thermals, a new ax, and a couple of cores to replace those in his guns. "We still have our jobs to do, but let's kick them off our lawn first."

CHAPTER TWENTY-SIX

"This is the slowest elevator I have ever used." Kaiden sneered and tapped his foot impatiently against the floor as the hum continued while the elevator descended to the bay below.

"Not to mention that it's a little cramped in here." Cameron grunted and leaned closer to the wall as a security guard's elbow continued to dig into him. "Did we really all have to pile in here?"

"There was only one elevator." Haldt shrugged. "Most people don't use this entrance. It was hard to convince anyone that we needed a spare."

"We seem to be in a rather disadvantageous situation should anyone attack," Genos pointed out and examined the rickety and slipshod container. "Even weak weapons could reach us through the glass of the door."

"We'll get down there eventually," Jaxon said calmly from where he leaned against the side of the box. "I doubt there'll be too many threats and didn't see any signs of damage or struggle in the lobby."

"The droids seem persistent and willing to use more untraditional paths," Genos insisted. "We should still be on guard."

"Agreed, but it'll be a direct route into the hangar once we reach the bottom, so there shouldn't be too many surprises left," Haldt reasoned.

"I'm surprised you're as hopeful as you are considering how today has gone so far," Kaiden muttered.

"You have to keep your head up otherwise, you get lost in the chaos," the officer replied.

Chiyo activated the tablet on her wrist. "When we get down there, I'll send a directive to all your EIs to search for — Wait, do you hear that?"

Kaiden looked up and listened. Over the creaking of the elevator and hum of machinery, he heard the sound of rushing air. It was faint and seemed to come from the distance, neither above nor below them.

"That sounds like something flying at high speed—maybe a drone?"

"Too fast." Cameron countered and readied his rifle. "That's a rocket."

Kaiden looked over as the front of the elevator finally descended past the rocky walls and revealed a massive interior hall with tall ceilings. Below them, looking up with glinting blue eyes, were a dozen Arbiter bots.

"So much for them not being down here," the bounty hunter shouted as he kicked the glass of the elevator out, took aim, and fired at the rocket. Thankfully, his aim was true and he destroyed it before it could hit them.

Kaiden clenched his teeth and readied his weapon.

"Assholes. At least wait for us to get out of the elevator before you try to blow us up."

"I doubt machines have much of a sense of honor. If they see an opportunity to attack, Kaiden, they will take it." Jaxon tried to aim at the droids below. "I can't get an angle at this height. Everyone back up and wait until—oh no. They're gonna shoot the hover line at the bottom."

"Everyone get close to me!" Eckles ordered. He pounded his fists together and a bright purple light burst from his gauntlets. An explosion rocked the elevator and it plummeted but a large purple sphere appeared around the group barely seconds before impact.

Fortunately, the barrier broke their falls before it shattered. The two aces rolled forward and kicked what remained of the doors open. Another rocket careened toward them but Haldt destroyed it with a single shot as soon as he had visual. Kaiden took a thermal out and activated it, lobbed it at a trio of bots that immediately scattered before it detonated, and bought the group time to recover.

"Is everyone all right?" he asked and helped the others to their feet.

We're good. That was quick thinking," Haldt commended and joined him and Jaxon at the front to confront the bots that blocked their path.

"It is quite fortunate for us that you are a vanguard," Genos acknowledged as Eckles helped him up.

"Technically, I'm a soldier. I only tinker with different gadgets from time to time." Another rocket was fired by one of the droids, although this one went wide as Jaxon shot the droid's arm off before it launched. The missile pounded into a nearby wall. "I can go into more details later."

Genos nodded. "That is a good idea."

"Genos, charge your cannon!" Kaiden yelled. The Tsuna nodded, dropped his rifle, and drew the cannon. As he began to charge it, the ace snagged another thermal but didn't activate it before he tossed it to the left of two of the hostile droids. They didn't seem to notice that it wasn't armed and both dashed to the right to escape it. Genos saw his opportunity and fired a charged blast at the two. One looked up in time to see the glowing orb barrel down on them.

They were both caught in the explosion and their forms melted and disappeared in the flash of red.

"Dammit!" The ace looked back to see one of the guards struggling against a rather agile droid. He ran to the unexploded thermal and paused as the mechanical armed its cannon with another rocket and turned to fire at him. Without a moment to spare, he slid down and snatched the grenade, pressed the button to activate it, and held it to let the explosive cook.

As the droid lined up his shot, his rocket launcher was knocked away by a shot from Cameron's sniper rifle. Kaiden used the opportunity to lob the grenade at it. The mechanical tipped backward in an effort to avoid it but the device exploded in its face. It was blown into the wall as the force of the blast shattered its shield and severed its left arm and leg before it caved its head in. The mechanical slid onto the floor, sputtering, and the right arm twitched until it finally stopped moving.

"Good riddance." Kaiden nodded to the guard, who

turned his attention to helping to finish off the small group of droids. He ran over to Haldt. "If these guys got in here, there's a good chance more will soon."

"Agreed. Let's hurry." The two broke away from the group and ran down the long corridor to the hangar door.

"Good Lord, who were they trying to impress?" the ace grunted as they drew closer.

"Supplies and parts come through here as well," the security officer explained and gestured to some of the doors at the side. "But I'll admit it does seem a bit much."

"You do have the codes to get in, right?"

"Of course, but that may not help much," he admitted.

"What do you mean?" He tilted his head in confusion when his companion pointed forward. The door to the hangar had been largely destroyed, most likely by the droids when they arrived. The ace drew his weapon. "Do you think they got in?"

"I would be ready just in case, but my guess is that we would hear explosions inside when they destroyed the ships if they were in there." They reached the doors and Kaiden tried to check inside through the cracks while Haldt punched in the code to open it. It started but a loud screech announced the fact that the doors were unable to move apart from each other more than a few inches.

"Dammit. Do you have any more explosives?" the ace asked. Despite having the spare thermals Jaxon had given him, he wouldn't have enough to blow through the doors, even with them as damaged as they were.

"I have something better." Haldt stepped to the side and gestured for him to do the same as he placed a couple of fingers on the side of his helmet. "Eckles, do you think you can help us with these doors?"

From the other side of the corridor, Eckles pushed into a sprint toward them. His armor began to glow again and the purple light seemingly sparked out of areas like the legs and shoulders. Kaiden realized what he was doing and decided to take more than only a couple steps back as the man bulldozed into the door without even slowing. The energy surged and hurled one of the doors down and the other inside by several feet.

The other two men ran to help him up. "Did that work?"

"It worked damn well," the ace replied with a chuckle. "Are you all right?"

"Yeah, but using that much energy back to back has me tapped for now," Eckles stated as he stood.

"That's fine. We're in now," Haldt said as he peered into the bay at the waiting ships. "Let's get everything ready. We need to get these ships into the air and sea."

As the ace scanned the ships, a thought occurred that should have come to him sooner. "Haldt, don't you think the ships will be shot out of the air?"

"The shields will hold against the droids' guns. The mechs might be trickier but we have good flyers." He took a tablet out. "I need to get them here now that we have a route—"

"And the big-ass ship in the sky?" he questioned as the others finally joined them.

The security officer raised his head. "Wolfson told me Laurie was handling it. But if he needs a hand, I have access to some real firepower down here. But that's a last resort.

It may be too hopeful to think we can actually destroy that thing, but on the off-chance that we can, do you really want it to crash into the island?"

Kaiden frowned as Genos, Jaxon, Chiyo, and some of the security team hurried away to begin prepping some of the ships. "At this point, if it guaranteed that those bastards went down with it, I honestly might."

"After everyone got off the island of course?" Haldt questioned.

Kaiden nodded, albeit with a little less enthusiasm than he normally showed. "Yeah, of course."

CHAPTER TWENTY-SEVEN

"Is everyone in position?" an officer asked.

"Most of them are still busy in the plaza," a recruit responded. "The ones that are still here are in position, but they're not great locations. We'll have to lead these droids into the center area."

"You make it sound so easy," another recruit muttered as he took his empty magazine out and reloaded. "Have they got through the doors yet?"

"Two of them so far and I'm about to take down a third," a security guard said. "After that, it's only the one in front of us."

"How many do we have left?" the ensign questioned and scanned the area.

"Twenty-eight of us and about forty bots," a petty officer responded and nodded approval as several security bots positioned themselves immediately behind the barrier.

"Wolfson will be here soon, right?" Before anyone could answer, the doors ahead of them erupted. Several Ark soldiers stepped forward, flanked by a large group of droids.

"They're here already!" a recruit shouted.

"Fire! Get them into the center," the ensign ordered as he raised his machine gun and fired.

One of the soldiers pointed forward and the bots attacked first, firing around the soldiers or leaping over them to attack the guards. The others began to push forward and picked off any target they could.

The guards and Arbiter forces clashed, accompanied by a loud banging noise from down the hall. One of the security officers gaped when a mech walked in, barely able to fit through the entrance before it lumbered over to the battle.

"Mech!" a recruit shouted before a blast burst the top of his helmet and head open.

As it raised one of its cannons to fire, a window shattered above it and Wolfson dove from two floors above, his arm glowing as he fell toward it. When he slammed the gauntlet into the top of the machine, a bright light erupted and hurled almost everyone in the fight off their feet. The walls began to crack and every window shattered around them.

Some of the guards recovered quickly and eliminated the briefly disabled droids while the Ark soldiers stared in shock as the once-great mech now had both its head and chest flattened. The arms were severed and sprawled on opposite sides of the hall.

One of the invaders looked at his teammates. "Who the hell was tha—ugh!" A heat-blade ax, tossed from the smoke surrounding the mech, buried itself into the back of his head. As he collapsed, Wolfson walked out of the smoke with a charged cannon aimed at the soldiers. "I'm Head Officer Baioh Wolfson," he shouted, his aim unwavering and his face stony. "Get the hell out of my building and off my island, idiots."

He fired the cannon and a ball of energy sailed directly toward the soldiers. They flung themselves hastily aside, but the orb impacted a droid behind them and released a wave of energy that destroyed their shields as well as a couple of other droids nearby.

The head officer took a thermal out, activated it, and rolled it across the ground while he charged another shot in his hand cannon with his other hand. One of the Ark soldiers lunged to catch the thermal to hurl it back, but as he raised his arm to throw, Wolfson fired his weapon at the explosive and it detonated in the soldier's hand to obliterate him and half of an Arbiter bot that crawled next to him.

The soldier who had signaled the others to attack began walking toward Wolfson and ordered the others to continue the fight as he did so. The giant aimed his cannon at the challenger and fired. The soldier pressed a button on his belt that seemed to strengthen his shields as they went from almost translucent to a bright blue. The charged shot struck solidly, and the man slid back but did not fall. His shields were clearly gone, but he simply took aim and fired at the head officer.

Wolfson managed to retain his cannon as he dove out of the way of the machine gunfire. He landed behind a pillar but heard a loud click from the soldier's direction, one he was familiar with. It indicated rounds switching in a weapon, usually to a heavier caliber. He pushed off the pillar as two ballistic shots impacted the metal plating and drilled through. Before the invader could initiate a follow-up attack, he turned and fired his hand cannon to force the soldier back. The man also dropped his rifle hastily when one of the shots grazed the chamber and ignited the shots inside. He tossed it away before it could erupt in his hands.

The security head prepared to make the final shot at the soldier but his gun was shot out of his hand. He muttered and looked over to locate the culprit. One of the other Ark soldiers had made a hurried shot at him from above despite the fact that he was harried by security bots and had probably intended it for his head.

The enemy he was fighting brandished a long, curved plasma blade that looked more like a machete. He twirled it as he stalked closer.

Wolfson took his spare ax out and pressed the switch to heat the blade as he motioned for the soldier to attack. His adversary took the bait and charged the giant, who simply drew his arm back and hurled the ax into his attacker's skull. Momentum carried the body for a few steps before it fell limply and slid over to his feet.

The officer stooped, grasped the hilt of the ax, and pried it loose from the soldier's skull before he turned to help the others. He checked the energy level of his force gauntlet as he stowed the ax.

Satisfied that he had what he needed, he nodded as he activated the switch on the gauntlet once more and jogged toward the center of the fighting. His armor and shields held up easily against the droids that fired at him. "You boys and girls had better brace for this!" he shouted and the security teams broke away from the battle as he leapt up and came down hard to pound his fist into the ground. The resulting eruption annihilated the remaining Arbiter bots.

"Come on...down here." Dr Soni ushered another patient through the hatch. "Dr Calloway, is everyone down?"

"We're only waiting on you and our rescuers to get down here," he called in response.

"We'll be right down," she promised before she turned and smiled at Amber. "Thank you for coming for us."

"Of course." Her daughter nodded. "But we're not out of here yet. We need to get into town." She looked down the hall to where Flynn and Marlo stood guard. "Are you guys coming?"

"You two head on down first," the marksman responded and held her gaze. "We'll follow."

Amber nodded and Dr Soni continued down the shaft. Once she was halfway down, the battle medic took her place on the ladder and called to her teammate. "Flynn, you should call Kaiden and tell him we're all right."

Flynn looked from her to Marlo. "I guess we should let him know what's going on. He probably wants to stay and fight all the droids."

The demolisher chuckled as he turned to enter the room. "Yeah, no—what's that?"

The students turned as several figures in dark armor appeared from around the corner with their weapons at the ready.

"It looks like we found who took out the droids," one of them muttered and aimed his rifle.

"Flynn, get out of here!" Marlo yelled as he fired a beam from his cannon. The soldiers were able to get back in time to avoid the blast, but one fired a dart from their gauntlet that struck Marlo in the chest. He staggered to the side and slid against the wall as the chemicals in the projectile made their way through his system.

"Marlo!" Flynn called and glanced back as Amber crawled out of the tunnel. "Amber, get out of here."

"Flynn, don't!" she shouted as he thumped the heel of his palm on the door panel to lock the pathway door and force the hatch shut. She was forced to climb down again and heard several shots go off before the hatch closed fully and locked.

CHAPTER TWENTY-EIGHT

D ario walked into the dimly lit hallway and sent a message on his tablet that the reinforcements had arrived and were already joining the main force and that he was on his way to take care of the other thing.

The timing was excellent, considering the massive number of ships that had appeared around the cloud city.

According to his current count, there were five battle-ships, two destroyers—formerly three—and four dread-naughts, plus all the cruisers that usually accompanied the much bigger vessels. Things had become a little claustro-phobic, but they wouldn't threaten the main building yet. They had to confirm hostages and try to make them stand down and surrender—much like what he imagined was happening at Nexus right now, only in reverse.

The assassin wasn't too concerned. He still had alterna-tives should everything go awry, but he felt confident. After all, he had already succeeded in infiltrating and damaging the supposedly impenetrable World Council— granted, with some help—so he could find a way around a few ships with the power to destroy entire stations in a matter of minutes that hovered outside his door.

And right now, he had a way—or, rather, a choice they had to make.

He slid the card into the panel and the door in front of him opened into the main power chamber. It closed behind him as he tossed the keycard to the side and walked down the steps to the central terminal, a giant glowing orb held in place by several tethers inside a shielded cage hung above him. This was Terra's original power core. It certainly wasn't the greatest design, despite the fact that it was able to accomplish getting the first cloud city airborne. The disadvantage was that it had the potential to be rather destructive if not handled properly. It had been replaced by an arc-link system over time but they couldn't exactly safely dispose of a core like that and besides, it could always be used in case of emergency.

Dario felt this was an emergency and he felt most of the WC would agree with him, although only technically.

Footsteps behind him gave him pause and he looked back at a man—probably a military staffer—who aimed a gun at him. There was dried blood on the arm of his dress shirt and the side of his head.

"Well, hello," the infiltrator said cheerfully and turned fully toward him. "How did the bots miss you?"

"What the fuck do you think you're doing?" the man yelled and his finger slid along the trigger of the gun.

He folded his arms and leaned back. "Now or at the beginning of the day? One is actually easier to explain."

The man's expression became instantly enraged at the casualness of this uncaring response. He tightened his finger on the trigger of the gun and took a step forward as he bristled with fury and indignation.

"Listen, you fucking prick. Do you know what you've done—how many of my teammates and friends you've killed today? Fuck you!" He held the rifle with one hand and drew his knife with the other. "I don't know what you think you've accomplished, but this kind of terrorism will be answered in kind. All you have done is earned the wrath of the entire planet. You will be made to take punishment for birthath hava koleth—"

His words jumbled in his throat and he began to taste a metallic liquid. Startled, he felt his mouth to see what was wrong and why he couldn't seem to speak. He slid two fingers into his mouth and his eyes widened. Sweat appeared on his face and trickled down to his throat when he realized he had no tongue and that the liquid that filled his mouth was blood.

He spat the puddle of blood out quickly and startled when something clanged noisily on the floor at his feet. Unbelievably, his knife had fallen beside him and more blood dripped from it. He frowned when he realized that the drips came from above it.

Shaking, he raised the arm slowly and recoiled when he saw that the hand that had held the blade was gone, replaced by a bloody stump that appeared to have been cut clean through by a razor. Before his mind could make sense of it, he collapsed and fell hard chest-down but flipped quickly to see both legs gone, severed above the knee.

Now in a full-blown panic, he used his one remaining arm to drag himself along. A trail of blood spurted from his lost legs. When he felt something behind him, he looked up at the assassin, who smiled.

"You know, I was having such a pleasant day up until now," he murmured before he kicked the once defiant man away. He recovered and attempted to crawl away. While he didn't understand what was happening, this man had to be the reason and he had never feared anyone or anything as much before.

Dario walked beside him for a while and simply observed before he drove his boot into the man's hand and stopped him. His victim shrieked a garbled cry before he caught his breath and looked slowly at his assailant. The assassin knelt, removed his foot from the pitiful man's hand, and gave him a slow, devilish smile.

"You may be right, one day, on the whole having to answer for my crimes and all that. But for now, all you have accomplished is to make me waste two hundred and seventy-eight nanos."

He raised a finger with a glowing orb at the tip and settled it next to the man's ear before he stood and walked over to the console. Casually, he slid a device into one of the slots and began to type.

"I killed many of your friends, you say? I've killed many people's friends. I've actually wondered if I should keep a separate tally for that category," he mused as he pressed one last key and the console began to upload. "As for the World Council, I'm not the one with the issues against it. That would be my boss, who is much more proactive than I am. In another life, he might have been a great council member." The man could barely hear him now, having lost too much blood.

"At this point, what happens next isn't up to me anymore," he admitted as he knelt beside the man and smiled once again as he raised his hand with his thumb pressed against his middle finger. "No more than living is your choice now." He snapped his fingers and the man's eyes rolled into the back of his head.

The assassin stood and sighed. He had been somewhat dramatic, he acknowledged. Not to mention that, while normally two hundred and seventy-eight nanos was close to nothing, he had used them rather liberally since the attack and was out of spares. He needed to be more conservative until he returned to his ship. The thought brought a frown. Holding back was not his favorite necessity.

He received another warning on his tablet. Two more battleships had arrived. Thus far, the ships had dispatched troops to assist with the fight on the ground. They would grow tired of this tactic soon enough and would decide that a building—and the people within—could be replaced and therefore sacrificed to repel the invaders. He did not intend to be around once that particular decision was made but he would speed the process up.

The upload had finished, and Dario watched the orb inside the machine begin to descend into the depths. It would still take several hours before everything would be in place. He'd stick around until then, but he would be sure to get out when the time came and find a suitable viewing point.

He wanted to see what it looked like when a cloud city was forced back to Earth.

CHAPTER TWENTY-NINE

"We made it," Izzy shouted as the group of Nexus students and faculty saw the double doors at the end of the tunnel.

"We should still be ready," Julius warned as he and Otto helped officer Malcolm to increase the pace. "The attacks seem focused on the Academy, but I'm sure they wouldn't leave the city undisturbed."

"We haven't heard anything from the police force." Malcolm grunted and nodded to Otto and Julius to let him stand on his own. "Try to reach them on the terminal at the door first. We don't want to rush into the waiting arms of those things after we managed to escape them."

Indre nodded. She, Izzy, and a handful of students approached the terminal and she glanced over her shoulder as she activated it and selected the comms channel to the Bellingham police department.

Several seconds passed with no reply before the connection died. Murmurs of unease rippled through the group until a messenger popped up.

Standby, doors will open shortly.

"They didn't answer the call," Indre commented and prepared her weapon. "Could this be a trap?"

"Maybe their commlink is down," a student suggested. "All of ours were until a few moments ago."

"Everyone, stand back," Malcolm ordered as the latches on the door slid back. "The doors are opening."

The group took several steps away from the exit, hopeful but hesitant as the doors began to open. Light poured in from the other side where several figures stood waiting for them.

All wore police and medic uniforms.

"We have another arrival from Nexus," one of the cops said into a comm as the group helped to usher the Nexus students into the emergency shelter.

"It's good to see someone friendly after all this." Indre sighed as she walked in to take a seat on one of the benches.

"I wouldn't get too relaxed," a medic replied as she bent to examine the agent. "There's fighting going on above in town."

"How bad is it?" Otto asked. "Many of us are in shape to fight if you can provide weapons."

"That's not the protocol," one of the officers replied.

"This isn't really normal circumstances," Izzy countered and refused to relinquish the pistol she had when one of the officers looked at it. Fortunately, the man stepped away quickly to indicate that he wouldn't attempt to disarm her.

The lead officer helped Julius take Malcolm to one of the beds. "It's weird to say it like this but compared to the

Academy, the fighting here has been almost pedestrian considering the initial strike on the island we saw."

"It looked like you would be obliterated almost immediately," Indre's medic added and handed her an energy tab. "Those pods—we thought they were bombs for a minute there. The police force scrambled to go and assist but then we came under attack only a few minutes after you did."

"We feared the worst when our messages didn't go through and the tunnels wouldn't open," the lead officer explained. "We now have confirmation that they have all activated again, so more of the staff and student body should be able to make it through."

"It depends on how many survived the attack," Malcolm reminded them as he eased himself onto the bed. "And the tunnels will automatically lock if unregistered forces try to enter. The idea was for evacuation before an attack could happen, not hours into one."

"It's what we trained for," Julius pointed out, although he grimaced after a moment. "Most of us, anyway. I worry about the first years."

"Did anyone see what's going on with that ship?" Otto asked and glanced at the ceiling of the shelter as if he could see the vessel through it. "Getting off the island is one thing, but we aren't exactly safe as long as a colossus hovers above us."

The lead officer frowned. "We're preparing shuttles and carriers for evac, as many as we can muster. The ship seems to have powered down slightly and some of the sections have deactivated. We haven't been able to determine why yet but we won't simply stand around and hope they have somehow hobbled themselves."

The security officer leaned up on his elbows and looked at the officer. "We have many more shuttles and ships to spare at Nexus, but I'm not sure if anyone has been able to reach them."

"Are we ready to go?" Eckles asked Haldt as they approached the elevator.

"I made contact with Corrin. She was able to find some of the other pilot students and teachers and they tried to make their way over here themselves but were pinned down at the observation center," he explained. "I contacted HQ as well. They still have any number of fires to put out but were able to get some of the other officers with pilot experience or talents into the tunnels. They should arrive here shortly."

"Are we going to help Corrin and the pilots?"

Haldt nodded as he walked to the left of what remained of the elevator they rode down on. He pressed a switch and a ladder descended. "We'd be more useful that way than simply standing around here. The others will get the ships ready and be on guard in case any of those droids come through."

His teammate nodded and grasped the ladder as the other man ascended. "Remember to keep your head down. We don't have shields for another fifteen minutes."

As the security officers continued their climb, Kaiden stepped out of the shuttle he had primed in the hangar.

Another officer climbed into the next vessel and the entire group bustled frantically to prepare the ships as quickly as they could.

He folded his arms as Chiyo stepped out of the shuttle next to his and approached him. "Is something wrong?" she asked when she saw his disgruntled expression.

"I'm only impatient." He sighed. "I know we can't get into the sky until more pilots arrive or we risk making the hangar a primary target, but at least a few of us here can fly. I feel we should be airborne already and helping the others."

"That's not the only thing, is it?" she pressed. He turned slowly to face her. "You're trying to come to terms with the fact that we have to evacuate."

He leaned against the side of the shuttle. "Evacuate, retreat, run away—I'm not saying I haven't had to make that choice in the past, but it never sat well with me. And this time? Shit, I see what we're up against and..." He trailed off, seemingly unable to get his words together, and she raised a hand and placed it against his cheek.

"I know you'll come back and I can tell you that I'm almost certain we'll come back. We won't let Nexus remain in their hands. And we will make them regret their actions."

Kaiden smiled and took her hand as he nodded and chuckled. "I guess I have something to look forward to now— after we get everyone out."

"Friends! I have almost completed my section!" Genos called from across the hangar.

The ace grinned at him with a mixture of surprise and

respect on his face. "Jesus. We only started about ten minutes ago."

"I wanted to tell you that I saw a few more ships in this chamber off to the side of the hangar," the Tsuna engineer informed them.

"That's where they handle repairs," one of the guards shouted. "There might be a couple ready to go in there, but the rest probably won't be in the best shape."

"I'll take a look," Kaiden offered and glanced at Chiyo. "Do you think you can get the others ready?"

"Of course." She nodded and he returned it before he ran over to Genos.

"Where did you say it was, Genos?"

The Tsuna scrambled out of his shuttle and pointed. "In this direction. There are a couple more shuttles in there that I have yet to inspect, but there was also another ship."

"Different than a shuttle?" he asked.

Genos nodded as they entered the repairs bay. "Certainly. This one actually has weapons and it seemed familiar. Maybe you can recall from where for me?"

The ace gaped and stopped in his tracks. It was indeed very familiar. He smiled as he clapped his friend on the shoulder. "Nice find, Genos, but I call dibs."

CHAPTER THIRTY

Lena puffed her cheeks out while she studied the readouts, something Nolan took notice of. He gestured to an officer to keep watch and walked down to the technician to lean over her shoulder. "Is something wrong?"

She shook her head and switched over to a screen showing the EIs' code. "No, it'll be fine. It's definitely complex and I would be shocked if any of your people could crack the EI. The professor certainly pulled out all the flash to make this one."

"And yet you sound disappointed," he stated as he straightened and took hold of her seat. "I thought you enjoyed a challenge, Lena."

"Oh, I do," she admitted, and her artificial eye dimmed slightly. "It's only that...I had really hoped we would get the special EI Sir Merrick has talked about all this time."

"I thought you had been briefed that it is no longer a primary target."

She nodded and drew her legs under the seat. "I was. Merrick told me it would probably take far longer and that I wouldn't need to crack it as he planned to simply extract it when he had the chance. Still, I kind of hoped all this fighting would bring it out of hiding."

Hiding? The general doubted that its user was hiding. Hell, for someone in obvious danger, this Kaiden Jericho almost seemed suicidal with how much he had poked the nest over the last couple of years. He had no doubt that the ace was down there somewhere. Lena and Merrick would eventually have their little pet project but for now, however, they needed the ship back at full capacity.

"Not to deprive you of your fun, Lena, but we need the ship to have an EI as soon as possible," he stated and tapped her shoulder. "We devised this plan because we had hoped to strip the professor of his EI to provide us with a better one and thus put them at an additional disadvantage. If this ship remains neutral for much longer—"

Lena held a hand up and nodded. She stood and retrieved the small glowing cube she had arrived with. "I'll head to the main lab. Cut all unnecessary power outputs and close any extraneous comm lines or linked devices. I'll bring the EI under our control soon."

Nolan watched her go and smirked as he moved to take his place in his seat. As he sat, he felt content—not safe or victorious, but he could see the pieces finally falling into place to build a path there. Lena would bring the EI to heel, and he would make sure that Nexus would follow suit.

Sasha lowered himself slowly down the side of the Animus Center, found one of the many broken windows on the third floor, and swung himself in. He retracted his grapple deftly and snuck into the hallway. When the enemy troops had arrived, most had simply fanned out and joined the carnage—except for this small group of six who moved immediately to the AC. He tailed them and fired at soldiers and arbiter droids along the way when he could do so without revealing his position.

Of course, he should focus on the defense of the Academy and the evacuation. That was his responsibility as chancellor now, but his instincts told him that this group wanted something in particular. A feeling of dread settled on him when he imagined them getting it, although he had little idea of what it was and what they planned to do with it.

He reached the middle of the hall and leaned over the edge to look at the lobby, where the group huddled around a holographic map. The commander used the zoom on his oculars to see where they were headed and grimaced when he realized that it was the mainframe. It should have been obvious as that would be one of the only places where they could plunder something useful. But even with that destination, he couldn't think of what they intended to take.

One of the soldiers looked around casually and the commander hunkered down to avoid notice. He had Isaac open the directory in his HUD. There were currently twenty-two people still in the building, although a few of them had darkened names, which indicated that they could not be reached by comms or that they were simply dead.

He heard the soldiers move out below and wondered if he should take the shot and end them there. Instead, he decided to follow. He needed to see what they wanted. If they were forced to leave the Academy in their hands, he intended to at least take whatever they were after with him.

He instructed Isaac to send a message to everyone in the vicinity to evacuate as hostiles were moving through the building. Although the fact that he had yet to see any droids or bodies indicated that this might, in fact, be one of the safest places currently on the island, it wouldn't remain that way for long once he eliminated these invaders.

"The first group of pilots is arriving," Cameron called into the hangar.

"That means we will head out soon," Jaxon told Genos, who nodded and made his way to one of the shuttles closest to the hangar bay doors.

"Are you set to go, Kaiden?" Chiyo asked over the comms as she walked to the back of the hangar. The pilots filed in and she motioned them toward the readied ships while she and one of the officers took control of the main terminal.

"Yeah, soon enough. Chief's looking for Wolfson's signature."

"I found him northwest of us. I think he's actually on his way to the armory like you thought," the EI confirmed. *"I can't get through to him, though. I think his comm is damaged as I only get static."*

"I'm sure he'll see us coming when we fly in." The ace chuckled as he settled the ship into a hover before he eased it toward the gates. "We are in his ship, after all."

"The pilots are in position," Jaxon advised. "The first group is ready to go—eleven shuttles and two water carriers."

"Haldt and Eckles sent orders to clear the harbor for the water carriers," Kaiden informed them. "Still, watch yourselves."

"We'll be fine," one of the pilots interjected. "We're in our element now."

"Thanks for getting them warm for us and clearing the way," another added. "It's time to use what we've learned over the last couple of years."

"Haldt gave me the code to activate the Academy's main guns," Chiyo reported. "Those should help keep the sky clear if they send fighters out to intercept. If they don't, we'll focus on eliminating the mechs."

"We'd appreciate it. Even first-year Nexus pilots can make these shuttles dance, but they don't have any weapons, unfortunately."

The infiltrator nodded and glanced at the guard beside her, who punched her code in as Chiyo punched in Haldt's. The guns came online and appeared on the top of several towers scattered along the island that most people would simply assume were decorative. As the cannons primed, she pressed the all-clear button and the hangar gates began to open—massive doors for the shuttles and one smaller door deeper in the hangar in a stream of water for the carriers.

"All right, guys, let's make this quick!" Kaiden hollered

as he prepared to boost out. "The sooner we get off the island, the sooner we can make plans to take it back!"

CHAPTER THIRTY-ONE

"These things are relentless," Cyra cried as two more of the R&D department's personal security bots fell to the Arbiter attack. A tech had his rifle snatched away from him by a retractable hook when an enemy jumped over the barrier, snagged him, and attempted to pull him away from his comrades.

Cyra and another techie hurdled their defenses to grab him and haul him back. She raised her pistol to shoot the droid and its eyes flared as it extended its cannon. In the next moment, something rocketed into it and hurled it away as the three techies collapsed and stared in shock. From behind, several dozen droids barreled down the hall and startled the techs and guards as they ran or bounded around them, forced their way through the barrier, and attacked the invaders.

Behind them, Professor Laurie walked calmly but resolutely toward them. "Cyra, everyone, we're going," he ordered.

"Professor!" she shouted, pushed to her feet, and darted

forward to engulf him in a hug. "Where did all these droids come from?"

He disengaged from her spontaneous embrace and withdrew a small rectangular device from his jacket, which he attached to the wall. "Failed experiments or prototypes. I had almost forgotten about most of them, to be frank. It wasn't until I smoked the databases and destroyed most of my tech that I remembered storing them in one of the extra rooms."

"Destroy— What is happening professor?" Cyra asked as he began to scan through numbers on the device.

"We're leaving. I...Aurora was able to temporarily cripple the flagship but at great cost. When it comes online again, I don't believe we'll have another opportunity to escape." He finished working on the device and clicked a button. After a brief hum, a massive rectangular light covered the wall and in an instant, the wall dissolved.

Laurie took several small pods out and tossed them below where they burst into gelatinous-looking blue spheres. "Out of the hallway, everyone. Please aim for the bubbles as this is not the time for broken bones."

"Professor, look!" Cyra pointed to one of the towers where the cannon was active.

"The cannons are online? Who activated them?" he demanded as several techies jumped out of the hole to the ground below. "Wolfson didn't say anything about activating them. Sasha? The only other place is the hangar—" At that moment, a shuttle flew past the R&D building and another turned quickly to land at the ground to pick up the technicians.

"We have shuttles now, it seems," he mused as he took

Cyra's hand. "And that answers my question as well." The two leapt down as the bots continued their rampage in the building.

"Sir, more are coming!" a guard shouted as another wave of bots approached.

"Keep them busy," Wolfson ordered but immediately reconsidered. "Actually, blast the bastards to pieces. And you two, get the armory open."

"It's in lockdown, sir. It needs your clearance," one responded. The head officer nodded and handed the man his shotgun as they changed positions. He punched in his faculty code and let the scanner read his eye. At a loud clanging above him, he drew his hand cannon and fired it toward the sound. A droid that had tried to climb down the building landed in a heap beside him, shot through the chest.

The terminal light turned green and the doors to the warehouse began to open. "All right! Everyone get in here." The six guards he was able to recruit along the way began to walk back, still firing. He joined the barrage with his hand cannon until the guard returned his shotgun, then fired with both as the team made their way in. Once they had all crossed the threshold, he fired at the terminal and forced the doors to slam shut.

"Everyone, get to work. Put all level three or below weapons to the left side for transport. Rig everything else," he commanded as he strode forward.

"Do you think that door will hold them for long

enough, sir?" one of the officers asked as another opened a crate of explosives.

"I doubt it, but don't worry about that," he responded as he walked deeper into the warehouse. "I made some personal acquisitions before the year started since I was gonna be trapped here and didn't want to fall out of practice. It looks like I've found a different use for these big boyos."

The guards all traded looks. "Big boyos, sir?"

"The skies are clear so far," Kaiden said and monitored the viewing feed from below the ship. "There is still a shit-ton of bots, though. Christ, we could probably build an entirely new academy using droid parts."

"*Watch your ass, Kaiden,*" Chief shouted as something rocked the ship. "*Or the ship's ass—stern, whichever.*"

"What the hell was that?" He flinched as he urged the ship forward and began to serpentine in the air in an attempt to avoid another shot like that one.

"*One of the mechs fired at us. We're all right, but I need to tinker with the energy outputs and focus on the shield. Otherwise, another couple of hits like that and we're through.*" With that, the EI disappeared from his view and appeared inside one of the monitors on the ship. He had begun to shut off nonessential systems when his eye widened. "*Kaiden, I detect known network codes nearby—Luke, Mack, Silas, and Raul.*"

"Really? Where?" he asked as he primed the ship's cannons. "It's time for some real air support."

"Is that the best you have, you son of a bitch?" Mack demanded as he hurled the Ark soldier into a pillar and actually forced him through it. The soldier tried to stand, but the vanguard snatched him up with the engineering claw, spun him around, and pounded him into the wall of the cafeteria.

"Mack, watch out!" Luke warned and threw his electrified rod like a spear at a bot that tried to sneak up on the vanguard. It landed to the right of its chest and the mechanical began to spasm while the two teammates began to put some distance between themselves and additional approaching bots, dodging orbs and darts along the way.

"Raul, Silas, where are you guys?" Luke called.

"I'm trying to not end up like Raul right now," Silas answered over the comms.

"The comms are working now?" Mack asked and retrieved his tablet hastily to check it. A second later, an electrified spike drilled through it. "Bastards!"

"Yeah, comms work, and Raul's been hit by one of those darts. Well, more than one, and he felt woozy with only one. He's out and I'm pinned down with the engineers."

Mack and Luke glanced back as more droids had joined the hunt. "We'll help you, but we'll also bring trouble of our own."

"We're all in this together, right?" the enforcer retorted.

Mack chuckled and checked his claw. "Sure enou— Holy hell!" A black, silver, and gray dropship flew directly over them and cannons aimed behind the two heavies who immediately picked up the pace when they began to fire.

"Howdy, gents," Kaiden said cheerfully as he obliterated the droids behind them. "It's nice to see some friendly faces."

"Kaiden?" the titan yelled. "Damn man, good timing. Silas is pinned down and Raul is drugged."

"Was that before the attack?" the ace asked jokingly before he banked toward Silas. "I see you, Sy... Wait, who are those guys in the armor?"

"Take them out!" the enforcer shouted.

"There's no need to say it twice." He fired at the Arbiter ranks, destroyed the mechanicals, and forced the soldiers to pull back, although a couple were caught in the cannon fire and blown to pieces for their trouble.

The ace opened the back and hovered close to the ground. Mack ran over and helped Silas carry Raul while Luke ran onboard. "Hey, do you have any weap—" Kaiden tossed him his machine gun and pistol. "Thanks!"

The titan handed Silas the pistol after he and Mack placed Raul on the bench. They fired at any approaching hostiles while the last of the engineers scrambled aboard and the craft made its escape.

"Nice ride, Kaiden." Mack laughed as he walked into the cockpit. "It's good to see a familiar face in all this mess."

"My same thought," the ace agreed as he flew off the island before he banked to the left. "We're not quite done yet, though. I gotta make one more stop."

"Where at?" the vanguard asked.

"To the ride's real owner."

CHAPTER THIRTY-TWO

The Arbiter bots continued to pound on the reinforced doors of the armory as the mech rolled up. With it was a group of Ark soldiers, curious as to why the droids seemed so obsessed by this one location.

"Do you think a group is holed up in here?" one of them asked.

"If there is, they have nowhere to run. Behind the warehouse is nothing but the bay," another replied.

One of them held a tablet up, connected it to one of the droids, and rolled back the saved footage. "It looks like they were pursuing some of the guards— Wait, look at this. One of them—that big one without the helmet—that's Wolfson."

"The head officer?" another asked. "The chancellor wanted to speak to him, didn't he?"

"He is a priority," the other said and stowed his tablet. "Preferably alive."

"Preferably?"

"I think the chancellor does not believe we will be able

to take him in alive. It would be better to eliminate him if nothing else," the fourth explained.

Two of the soldiers waved him away and approached the doors as they retrieved explosives. "We'll see about that. Everything up until now has been nothing more than a glorified— What is that?"

The source of their confusion was a rumble. They could feel it even over the mech as it prepared to fire. It felt like something charging directly toward them from behind the doors.

The armory gate catapulted free and flatted any droid that wasn't quick enough to get away. The mech fired but only struck a large shield. Behind the dust, three large mechs—all white with a blue Nexus stripe—stood in the opening. One raised its arm and fired a charged blast at the Arbiter mech. The head erupted instantly, and it fell to its knees and almost toppled on top of the soldiers. The Nexus mechs began to move forward. One took point with a large plasma blade that it used to swipe and hack through the droids that attempted to engage it while the other two fired on the mechanicals indiscriminately to leave small craters with each shot.

"What the hell are those?" One of the soldiers shuddered as she pushed to her feet. "I don't remember a brief on anything like that!"

"Quit whining and take them— " The soldier didn't manage to finish his order before a hail of kinetic rounds burrowed through his back. His shields and armor did almost nothing to stop them and rapid spurts of blood erupted from the wounds as he fell.

A figure emerged from behind the mechs, grinning

madly with a chain gun in his hands. His beard and hair were matted with blood and one good eye scanned the battle. "More of you, eh?" Wolfson chuckled and held the trigger down. "That's fine by me. You'll keep me entertained while my team gets their work done."

Back at the Animus Center, another group of Ark soldiers made their way into the mainframe chamber. One looked up from their tablet and pointed deeper into the room.

"Are they both back there?" another asked.

The scout nodded. "The codex will be in the main terminal. One of you can get that. The Master EI will be in its own chamber deep in the back. They only use it for larger Animus projects like the Death Match."

"Understood."

"You didn't have to reply. I'm not the squad leader," the scout muttered.

"It wasn't me."

"Me either." The group looked at one another and shrugged or shook their heads.

"Then who the hell—" Four shots rang out a split second before four bodies fell.

The scout was stunned. In one infinitesimal moment, half his team was dead. In the next, someone dropped from above, dug a blade into one of the soldiers, and drew a pistol to shoot another. The remaining man was finally able to react and aimed hastily with his rifle, but he only managed to fire a single shot before the marksman yanked his blade out and flung it at him. It caught him through the visor and he stumbled and leaned on one of the servers before the attacker shoved his pistol under the soldier's helmet and fired, letting the body fall as he turned to the scout.

He tried to reach for his weapon, but the sniper snatched his hand and twisted, breaking a couple of fingers in his haste, which made the scout retch as he was thrust into another server. "Why do you need the codex and Master EI?"

"Like hell I'm going to tell you!" He winced when another finger was broken. "I won't break that easily. And you don't have the time for torture, do you?"

Sasha tilted his head and placed his pistol under the scout's chin. "You are right, I don't." His expression cold, he pulled the trigger and shoved him aside. He holstered the pistol and vented his rifle as he placed it on his back, although his pistol was instantly back in his hand when he heard the doors behind him open. Hastily, he aimed it upward once he recognized the newcomer. "Head Monitor Akello."

"Commander? I got your message and wanted to help but, uh…" She lowered her weapon when she noticed the bodies littering the floor and looked from them to Sasha. "I guess you didn't really need reinforcements, huh?"

"Actually, your assistance would be most appreciated," he admitted and gestured to the central terminal. "I need to remove the codex. While I'm doing that, will you transfer the Master EI to a more manageable device?"

"The Master EI?" she asked, although she soon realized that this wasn't the time for long explanations and simply nodded and moved toward the back. "There should already be a specialized EI drive for such situations. I have access to it. I'll get it done."

"Thank you. These grunts were here to retrieve them for some unknown reason and I don't want to leave them here for them to use later," he explained as he activated the terminal and began to eject the codex.

"I've received scattered reports and heard that they are abducting students as well."

Sasha nodded grimly, although he did take a moment to look at the soldiers he had slaughtered. "If this is the best they can offer, no wonder they want our students instead."

CHAPTER THIRTY-THREE

As the shuttle took them into the city, Laurie could not tear his gaze away from the colossus as if he expected it to reactivate at any time and turn everyone to glass in an instant. He looked into the case he had with him. Nestled within were a few different devices he'd decided were worth saving and two drives, each filled with all the data he could cram into them. One had almost two decades worth of research and tests, theories he had worked on, and experiments he had planned. The other was a replica of the Animus OS to restart the system once they hopefully returned.

It was oddly humbling to see all that work crushed into two small objects he could hold in one hand.

Cyra leaned over and placed a hand on his shoulder. He turned and smiled to thank her for the small kindness as he put the drives away and closed the case.

"Laurie, are you safe?" a voice asked from his tablet. His smile widened as he took it out.

"Sasha, it's good to hear from you," he responded and

glanced around the shuttle at the other passengers. "I'm quite safe now. Shuttles are going around the Academy to pick up whoever they can."

"That's good to hear," the commander admitted with a long sigh. "I'm at the Animus Center. A group of enemy soldiers came here to try to take the codex and Master EI."

"Do what?" he demanded, his head tilted in confusion. "Why would they need either of those?"

"I'm not sure. I'm with the head monitor and we're preparing to take both with us. I hoped you'd be able to shed some light on that."

"I honestly have no real answer," he said and crossed one leg over the other. "The codex has all the personal Animus information of the students. I'm not sure what they could do with that. It wouldn't really be any different from simply accessing their private files. Unless they are on the same Animus update we are, but even then, it would be no better than statistics, really."

"I suppose I'll have to let you take a look once we meet," Sasha reasoned. "As for the Master EI, from what I overhead of their discussion, they seemed to know what we use it for but didn't know why their leaders wanted it exactly or weren't willing to divulge what they did know."

"I see. If you can, please bring me a helmet or tablet from one of the soldiers. I'm sure there's something in there we can use. And once you bring me the Master EI and we have a powerful enough system to run it, I'll dig into the guts of it to see if it's hiding anything."

"Do you think that's a possibility?"

"At this point, I feel that there many things I'm unaware of—more than I used to think," Laurie muttered.

"And when it comes to the Master EI, I wasn't the only one who designed it."

The shuttle rocked slightly and he and everyone else looked out to see if they were under attack, but it appeared to be nothing more than a quick evasive maneuver to dodge some of the shots from below. The professor drew a sharp breath and continued. "One more thing, Sasha—we need to think about really evacuating. Not merely into town but a place that would actually make that colossus think twice about attacking."

"I know. I hoped we could at least have as many people together before we set out but time is of the essence." The commander was silent for a moment. "We'll leave many behind as well. Dammit. Listen, Laurie, when you get there, I need you to tell the police chief what will happen."

Wolfson continued to laugh as he fired his chain gun in waves from side to side. The tactic caught any bots that attempted to approach him. Any of the soldiers who tried to return fire quickly found themselves either under assault by another fusillade of bullets or were now a target of the mechs once they emerged from cover.

"Sir, we're almost ready!" one of the guards shouted behind him.

He looked back. "Really? I'm beginning to think we should simply keep going." He lifted his finger from the trigger and let the weapon cool for a moment as he turned to the guard. "At this rate and with these magnificent mechs on our side, we might actually take the Academy back!"

Two large blasts from behind the head officer made both he and the guard whirl to face the new threat. One of the mechs fell as four Arbiter mechs approached the warehouse. The other cannon mech fired and eliminated one but immediately earned retaliatory fire from the remaining enemy. The melee mech also had difficulty as a couple of dozen arbiter droids took the opportunity to crawl over it, rip into its armor, and fired at close range.

"Damn. I might have been a little over-eager," Wolfson muttered, raised his gun, and gestured to his team. "Activate the emergency shield. The doors aren't an option anymore."

"Right away, sir!" As one guard ran to comply, another approached.

"Sir, the weapons are ready to load, but where will we take them?" she asked.

He stared in surprise. "What? My ship hasn't arrived yet?" He put the chain gun down and retrieved his tablet. "I called it over here before I headed out there so it should be close enough for me to summon from here—what? It's heading this way but it's on manual." He growled a low oath as he pressed a few buttons on the tablet and connected to the comm in the ship. "Okay, who the hell is in my ship?"

"Could it be anyone else?" Kaiden responded, and in an instant, Wolfson's mood brightened.

"Kaiden! It's good to hear from you, boyo." He laughed. "Heard about the work you did at the docks. Nicely done! And I see you made it to the hangars."

"With help from my friends and Haldt's team," the ace confirmed. "I'm coming in. Are you ready to go?"

"It's good of you to think about me in all this mess." At a thud behind him, he turned to see a single droid shooting at the shield, but more were coming. The guard stood at the ready and looked at him for orders. "Say, Kaiden, we have weapons ready to go here but we may not have the time to get everything loaded. You wouldn't happen to have extra hands aboard, would ya?"

"As a matter of fact, I most certainly do," Kaiden replied. "Open the bay. Let's load up the toys and get your big ass out of there."

"Roger that." Wolfson stowed the tablet and gestured for the guard behind him to open the loading bay doors as he hefted his chain gun. "All of you back there, get the crates on the ship!" he ordered and readied his weapon once more.

The ace coasted the ship into the landing zone. When he opened the rear platform, Luke, Silas, Mack, and the four remaining engineers scrambled out. The engineers helped the guards move the crates onto the ship while the soldiers each found a weapon in the armory and stood beside Wolfson, ready to hold the droids at bay.

"It's good to see you, Wolfson," Luke said cheerfully. He held a titan hammer and attached a shielding gauntlet to his left arm. "And it's even better to have a real weapon again."

"No kidding." Mack chuckled and primed a cannon.

"Do you boys think you should be here?" the head officer asked somewhat sarcastically as he nodded to the shield which had begun to shatter beneath the barrage from at least thirty droids now firing at it. "We don't have much room to fuck up here."

"What do you think we've done all day?" Mack asked.

Silas stepped up and aimed a machine gun. "Besides, this is what we trained for."

Wolfson smiled and pressed down on the trigger as the shield collapsed. "Damn right."

CHAPTER THIRTY-FOUR

A panel on the left of the mainframe's central console opened and a pentagonal device ejected. Sasha retrieved the codex that held all the Animus users' information. He placed it in the satchel on his belt and began to shut the mainframe down. "Akello, are you almost finished?"

"I'm transferring the EI now," she stated and her gaze darted from her screen to the drive she had prepared. "It will take a few minutes."

The commander nodded and drew his rifle. "Then I will keep watch and begin the deletion process in the meantime."

"Deletion? Of the Animus?" She looked surprised. "I can lock it out. Without any of Laurie's clearances, they won't be able to—"

"They seem exceedingly familiar with the system," he reminded her. "I assume these are the same people who have hacked into the system over the last few years."

"What?" Akello exclaimed. "Why wasn't I informed?"

He turned to reply but was prevented from doing so by a loud crack as the glass was shattered in the front of the building. The commander looked at the exit of the maintenance chamber. "Later. For now, complete your objective. Then, I'll help you get out of here."

"We'll both get out of here, right?" she asked and stepped away from the terminal to approach him.

"I'm sure I'll leave the building at some point," he replied dismissively.

"You know I mean the Academy, Sasha," she pressed.

He turned back to her. "There are still students being pursued or taken away. I am the chancellor now. Should I simply leave them to their fate?"

"You can help us get them back," she protested. "We won't simply give up the fight after today, will we? If they are kidnapping the students, they have a plan for them, right? We can rescue them. Or do you think it's better that we lose two chancellors in less than a day?"

Sasha made no answer but simply looked away and exited the room to deal with the new intruders, leaving her to her task. She was right, in a way, but it didn't make guilt or fear diminish.

It occurred to him that he had left the army so he wouldn't have to feel like this again.

Damyen smirked as he read the information on his tablet. "The general still hasn't taken control of the Academy?" He chuckled. "It's been a couple of hours since we talked. I assumed he would have found his stride by now."

"Chancellor, the second and third Ark division have reported in," one of his aides said. Damyen looked up from his tablet as he lounged on the bed in his personal quarters. "The second division has access to the target's codex. The third has secured the facility."

He smiled with satisfaction as he raised the glass of whiskey to his lips. "Well done," he murmured as he took a sip. "What news do we have from the first, fourth, and fifth?"

"The first hasn't reported since their last message. They said the resistance was heavy but that they were about to receive assistance from the droid support units," she informed him. "As for the fourth and fifth, they were able to make their way into the ships but it appears both vessels immediately began to fly back to Terra once the alert was put out. They are still in the process of taking the ships over to delay them arriving at the capital where they could get reinforcements."

"They are heading to Terra, you say?" he enquired and thoughts began to form in his mind. "Remind me—how many ships do we have?"

"We have acquired fourteen WC military vessels. Along with the organization's personal ships available, we have a total of forty-two battleship or higher-class ships available."

"How many ships are currently circling Terra?" he asked.

"The last report was that there are currently a hundred and eleven, sir," she stated. "Merrick's agent Dario has already begun the destruction sequence."

The chancellor chuckled as he put the glass onto the

nightstand beside his bed and stood. "He got right on that, didn't he? Usually, he likes to play around more."

"He might be close to being overwhelmed at this point," the aide suggested. "The cramped quarters of the building have provided an advantageous position for the droids, but ever since the arrival of the research ship Galileo which had an entire compartment filled with weapons and devices specifically designed for automated combat, the tides have slowly turned. Not to mention the sheer enormity of numbers on the other side now that all the ships have begun to return."

"Let them keep throwing bodies if they want to," Damyen retorted and strode out of the room. His aide followed and snatched his jacket up on the way out. "Whether they die now or later is of little consequence to us. But I see an opportunity." He took the jacket from her and put it on. "Get me in contact with the leaders of the fourth and fifth. We could get a few more ships out of this if we play it right. There's no use in all of them going down in flames."

"Eckles, mech!" Haldt shouted and forced the pilot's head down as the vanguard bolted to his feet and activated a shield in the same moment that the mech fired its cannon. The shield blocked it but shattered and hurled the two security officers and the three pilots with them back.

"Shit!" Haldt cursed, scrambled up, and helped the others before they ran off while the mech charged another shot. "Corrin, is the path clear?"

"It is," the piloted responded over the comms. "Were you able to find the stragglers?"

"Of course we did." The group rounded the corner and crept through one of the back doors into the logistics workshop in an effort to avoid the mech. "Believe it or not, it was easier escorting the fifteen of you than the three of them."

"The mech stopped moving. It's simply standing there and looking around," Eckles whispered as he peered cautiously out of the door. "I don't think it will be easy to give it the slip."

Haldt activated the map in his HUD. "We could cut through the building, dammit. That would put us in the center of the plaza— wait, this is the logistics workshops, right?" Eckles and the pilots nodded and he scanned the map. "Chiyo, come in."

"I'm here, Officer Haldt," she responded. "The first ships have already been sent out. I see pilot Corrin and a squad coming in through the eastern entrance but I don't see you,"

"Yeah, that's what I'm calling about," he admitted. "I need you to take control of tower cannon three and turn it west toward the logistics workshop. You should see a mech."

"Should I destroy it?" she asked.

"If you would be so kind." No sooner had the request been made than they heard four large blasts rocket into the mech. Parts shattered and skidded across the ground from the power of the strikes. "Much appreciated. Do you mind walking us over to the entrance from here?"

"It would be for the best as it appears those shots

garnered a fair amount of attention. The cannons have been quite helpful but they are also prime targets. One, four, and six have already sustained moderate to heavy damage."

"It looks like we won't be able to rely on them for much longer," Eckles bemoaned.

Chiyo frowned and scanned the different feeds that showed that more and more of the campus was filled with droids and enemy soldiers rather than students and faculty. "We won't be able to stay here much longer either."

CHAPTER THIRTY-FIVE

"Wolfson, we're all loaded," Kaiden called from the back of the ship. "Get your ass in here."

"Easier said than done right now, boyo," the man roared as he continued to fire into the ranks of droids. Luke pounded the hammer down and a wave of energy erupted and forced the mechanicals back as metal bodies careened into their counterparts.

The ace looked back when the six officers all rushed out to help. He took one of the shotguns that protruded from the cases and joined them, holding onto the railing as he ushered them back onboard and obliterating any bot that came too close. "Chief, take us up."

"Got it, partner," the EI acknowledged and the ship began to hover above the platform.

"Turn and blast the bastards while you're at it," Wolfson ordered.

"I can do that too." The rear door began to close. Wolfson and Kaiden moved to the cockpit as the ship spun and released a barrage at the bots that continued to

fire. A few tried to leap onto the retreating craft but the security head took manual control even before he was fully seated. The sudden acceleration toppled Kaiden, along with some of the others who had yet to make it to their seats.

"Good timing, Kaiden," the giant said and slowed slightly when they were more than halfway across the bay. "So good that I won't even be angry you took my ship without asking me."

"Hey, I tried," the ace muttered as he stood and moved to take the co-pilot's chair. "Chief couldn't establish a connection with your comm."

"I guess I lost it in all the fuss." Wolfson chuckled and banked the vessel to head back toward the island. "I saw the guns your friends had—stopped by my gym, did you?"

"I made a quick pass through and was worried when I didn't see you there. You're always so sluggish in the mornings." Kaiden looked out the window at the destruction of the Academy. Several buildings collapsed and fires blazed on the right side of the island and through the docks. One of the tower cannons shorted out as several droids fell from it. "There will be a ton of work to repair it all when we reclaim it."

The head officer looked at his student and simply nodded in acknowledgment. "It's good to see you're still you through all of this."

"Did you think I would roll over for these assholes? I ain't gonna let them have that win."

Wolfson smirked. "You still had one year left but you've already learned the most important lesson for a soldier."

"You drilled it into me in the first couple," the ace

responded and leaned into the console. "We need to head back to the hangar. Chiyo and a few officers are still there."

"Are there no more pilots to get her out of there?" the giant asked.

"More are coming but I'd rather she was with me," Kaiden stated and the pilot simply nodded once again. "Fair's fair. You saved my ass so I should help you save your — What the hell is going on?"

The two men leaned forward as several of the pods the bots had arrived in began to ascend into the sky. "They weren't only landing pods?"

The head officers hold tightened on the control. "Sasha said the droids threw captured students into the pods."

"And they are heading back up—" He followed the trail of the vessels as they ascended to the colossus. "Shit."

***

"The first retrievals are on the way, sir." Nolan nodded to the technician.

"And the codex and Master EI?" he asked.

"The second team has been sent in, along with all bots in the sector to back them up. Whoever killed the first team will not leave alive."

The general leaned back in his chair. His mind had begun to slide into paranoia. What if they had already taken the codex and Master EI? Maybe the Academy had cut their losses and destroyed or deleted both to stop them from getting their hands on it. He drew a sharp breath and forced the feeling from his mind. No, he couldn't entertain the doubts—not now when he still had so much to complete. He would not fall to his neurosis again or let Merrick down.

"We should be prepared on the off-chance that they are unable to be retrieved," he stated and stood. "We have the professor's personal EI. Assuming Lena doesn't completely rewrite it, we should be able to use it to access the Academy's systems once the dust has settled. Make sure that they do not destroy the mainframe chamber. We'll need every trace of information that we can get." With that, the general left the bridge and directed his steps to the lab to check on Lena's progress.

When he arrived, over a dozen scientists and technicians were gathered around the monitor Lena was working on. Above them floated the cube she had arrived with, suspended in a tubular chamber.

"Lena? How is it coming along?" he asked and the group dispersed as he approached.

She didn't look up from the monitor and her fingers tapped madly on the keyboard. "It's been rather exciting—much more than I initially believed it would be," she replied. "I'm putting her back together now."

"Back together?" Nolan asked and stared anxiously at the cube. "You destroyed her?"

"It would be better to say unraveled," she corrected and took only a moment to glance quickly at the general before she turned her gaze to the cube. "She fought me the entire time and I had to take her code apart. It was basically bifurcating her artificial body to get her inside the cube. I'm putting her back together while the cube rewrites her. It's a much faster process."

"Then she'll be ready soon?" he asked.

Lena shrugged and one shoulder jutted when she craned her neck. "I hope so. I haven't had the time to familiarize myself with this device."

The general raised an eyebrow but kept his voice neutral despite the surprise. "Merrick told me that you use these to make our EIs."

"I use a different version. Besides, it is one thing to intertwine parts of EIs together, and another entirely to perfectly deconstruct and reconstruct an EI that was created by and the personal project of the creator of EIs."

Nolan eyed her warily before he walked to the side of the chamber to observe the cube from a different angle. "That sounds like you are preparing an excuse."

She stopped typing and stared at the general, her expression calm. "I'll have it ready soon. Laurie may be a genius, but he is not the only one."

He nodded and allowed a small grin to appear on his face. "Keep that confidence. I'm sure Merrick would approve."

Unsurprisingly, she made no reply and simply returned to her work. The general turned his attention to the rest of the staff. "The rest of you, get the pods ready. We'll have new recruits soon. Top-of-the-line, in fact."

"Does that mean we have the requirements ready, General?" one of the technicians asked.

Nolan approached him and linked his hands behind his back. "We have yet to acquire them but they aren't 'requirements,' merely preferable. Open the source code and play around with it for the time being."

The technicians looked at each other. The lead, whose tag read Keller, stepped forward. "Sir, trying to begin the process with simple guesswork could lead to irreparable damage to the subjects. If not outright death, mental shutdowns would be the most likely result."

He nodded and considered it carefully. "For now, get them in the pods and keep them in the system. We'll focus on retrieving the codex and Master EI, but if it comes down to it, I believe we can spare a few for you to experiment with." He walked away from the team and toward the door. "We'll need more soldiers soon."

When Flynn awoke, it wasn't for long. His mind drifted between reality and darkness and he blinked several times. Confused, he looked aroundbut all he could see were dark-blue lights. They seemed oddly familiar. He closed his eyes and opened them again. Now, the lights were white and almost blinded him. He heard a hum around him and a familiar feeling enveloped him as he leaned back and closed his eyes for a moment. When he opened them once again, he realized that he was all alone and suspended in darkness.

CHAPTER THIRTY-SIX

Sasha was able to crack the door to Animus hall seven open sufficiently to place both hands on the edge and push to force one side far enough for him to ease through. He could hear more soldiers approach and by the footsteps, he estimated three—no four. One wore light armor while the rest were in medium. He made his decision in seconds—separate them and eliminate the one in light armor, who would be the quickest and easiest target in the group. Thereafter, a few shots through the helmets of the others should finish this quickly. He glanced at Akello and pointed to a supply closest on the left where she could wait. She nodded and moved quickly inside it.

He retrieved his one remaining shock grenade and released a slow, measured breath before he slipped into the hall and slid the door closed behind him. As he made his way down one of the lines of Animus pods, the thud of the soldiers' boots a couple of lines over alerted him to the hostiles. He climbed one of the pods, used the railings to ascend toward the ceiling, and jumped across to catch the opposite rail with the sole of his boot to lessen the sound of his impact. In his new position, he paused to let the group pass him. They took the time to scan the room and even opened several pods. Their process told him clearly that this wasn't a team looking for hostages. It was a cleaning sweep.

When they were at the right range, he activated the shock grenade and lobbed it into the middle of the group and drew his rifle as it landed. The Ark soldiers saw it almost immediately and reacted accordingly. They flung themselves away from the electrical explosive as he took aim, but when he zoomed in through his scope, the vision blurred, and he felt the gun begin to overheat. *Shit, there is a hacker among them.*

"He's there!" one of them shouted. Sasha jumped down as they began to fire. He landed and immediately sprinted down the opposite line of pods. Two raced down the same path across from him. Instinctively, he went to draw his pistol but realized it was energy-based and probably also compromised. *Very well. This will get bloody.* He flicked his hand and his blade ejected from his gauntlet. Deliberately, he slowed his run enough to let the soldiers pass him. Both hurried to the end of their line to try to intercept him, unaware of the change in his position. He was almost level with them when the soldiers began to turn the corner. Before they could react, he bounded onto the last pod and used it to vault over their heads. They turned and fired but the shots went wide, and he plunged on top of them.

One of them tried hastily to correct his aim before the commander thrust his boot against his helmet. The kick hurled him into the Animus control console while Sasha spun and dug the blade into the other soldier's head. A surprised yelp was the only response before the body went limp. He yanked the blade out of the helmet, turned to the recovering hostile, and thrust his weapon into his neck. The man dropped his gun in shock and Sasha recovered it for himself and crouched as kinetic rounds fired overhead. He twisted and fired to catch the gunman in the knees. The soldier's leg armor gave way and he crumpled as Sasha pulled the trigger twice more. One shot damaged the soldier's helmet and the other pierced his head.

As the final armored soldier fell, Sasha stood. He raised his weapon and fired to his left in the same moment that a turret in the ceiling lowered to fire. This hacker might be skilled, but he was predictable.

"Isaac, scan for energy signatures," he ordered, but before he could locate the enemy, two shock grenades plummeted from above. He rolled out of their path and looked up. The hacker used the railings as he had but now ran away from the marksman. Smart but predictable and eager but a fool as well.

The commander took aim and fired. The kinetic round streaked through the invader's foot and he cried in pain and fell from the railings to land with a loud thud. Sasha darted toward him, reached the end of the seventh row of pods, and flattened his back against the one on the end to peer around the corner. Sure enough, several laser shots fired immediately. He caught a glimpse, though, of the hacker on his back, firing from the floor with his pistol aimed up a few inches. With his target located, he knelt, turned, and fired. The shot damaged the gun, which blew up in the soldier's hand.

The man uttered another cry of pain and held a shaking arm up. A holoscreen appeared. The hacker was persistent, he would grant him that. Sasha fired calmly at the man's gauntlet to deliver another strike at his armor. A small splatter of blood was followed by another wail and the holoscreen shorted out.

The commander scrambled to his feet and stalked toward the remaining soldier as he tossed the enemy rifle away. He caught the hacker by the throat and pressed his pistol against his head as he had with the scout earlier, "Are there more?" he questioned but received only a gurgled reply. "Why do you want the Master EI and codex?"

The man eyes could be seen through the amber visor and he seemed to study his adversary in the same way he studied him, "You'll find out. Even if you…make it out… they'll be our comrades…soon enough," was his only cryptic reply between deep breaths.

"Give me answers!" Sasha demanded and shoved his pistol against the left side of the helmet close to the jaw. "This can be quick or it can be slow and painful. But I will make that decision."

The hacker shook his head, but it wasn't necessarily a gesture of disagreement. It looked more akin to a spasm. "No, you won't. But I don't get to either."

As his captive rolled his head back, Sasha could see his hand inch toward his SMG. He sighed, fired, and let the man slump as he released him. He had to give them this, at least. They were dedicated to their cause—or possibly simply more afraid of the consequences of failure than death.

"Sasha, it's quiet now," Akello stated over the comms. "Is it clear to come out?"

"I'm not sure. I've eliminated four targets but I'm sure more are on their way or in other areas of the center," he stated and holstered his rifle. "I'll see if I can get us an extraction."

"Sir, I pick up more than fifty signatures headed in our direction," Isaac warned and displayed a map with numerous red dots that all seemed to converge on the Animus Center. From their readouts, it looked to be a group of droids rather than soldiers. He was sure the enemy knew that a number of their soldiers were dead now and grew either frantic or impatient enough that they would begin to tear the building itself apart to reach their objective. Sasha knew the Academy defenders wouldn't win this by being the last ones standing but by making sure the enemy didn't achieve their purpose. But what the hacker said disturbed him. He'd been specific to a degree—they would be their comrades. Logic insisted that he could only have meant the students or perhaps the military. Had he merely spouted nonsense to delay him?

He holstered his pistol, drew his rifle, and vented it. They needed to move higher and activate a beacon. "Akello, get to me. We're moving now."

CHAPTER THIRTY-SEVEN

"Hey, watch it," one of the pilots yelled over the comms.

Chiyo looked at the various camera feeds and tried to identify what had alarmed him. "What's the problem?"

"There's a dropship coming into the hangar. My readout says it belongs to the head officer of security."

"Wolfson's ship?" she asked and turned as the vessel sailed in and set down as the last four shuttles prepared to launch. She put her headset down and ran to it. The side door opened and Kaiden and a few security guards emerged before it had fully landed.

"Hey, Chi, how's it going?" he asked and scanned the once filled section quickly. "Most of the ships are out. Is Haldt back yet?"

"He went back to find any other pilots he could, but he should be on his way," she replied.

"Which way will he come from?" a guard asked and they ran to the east entrance tunnel once she gave them the direction.

"We're heading out soon. I came back to get you out as well," the ace stated and gestured to the ship. Luke stepped into the doorway.

"Hey, Chiyo!" he said with a wave. "It's still a little cramped in here but come on. It's gotta be better than staying here."

"You were able to find some of them?" she asked.

He nodded and held four fingers up. "Luke, Silas, Mack, and Raul, although he's still out of it. We found some engineers as well, a fairly decent pick-up for a quick run."

"Shit!" the guard at the central console yelled and thumped her fist into the device. "We lost another cannon."

"That makes three." The infiltrator sighed. "We won't have support for much longer."

"Do things still look bad out there?" Kaiden asked.

She nodded and rubbed a hand up her left arm. "Of course, but we didn't expect to turn this around anyway. The cannons allowed us to take out large swathes of droids and deal with the mechs easier, but they're systematically destroying them. The droids seem endless and the soldiers walking the grounds now seem to direct them as well to focus their attacks."

"Silas told me Raul said they had an insignia for the Russian Ark Academy," he informed her. "I don't know what the deal is, but I assume we're not the only Ark Academy involved in this fight."

"Hey, boyo!" Wolfson yelled. "We need to get moving. I have a distress call."

"From who?" the ace asked, his eyes narrowed.

"Sasha," Wolfson answered. "Our new chancellor is locked in the Animus Center."

"New chancellor?" Chiyo asked.

Kaiden shrugged. "He's the new chancellor? Wait, does that mean Durand is dead?"

The head officer's only reply was a beleaguered sigh, although it was enough of an answer for them to understand. "Dammit," the ace muttered. "Let's not lose another."

"Agreed. Get in here!" the giant bellowed as the ship primed once again.

He clambered into the side entrance and looked at the engineers. "You guys should wait for the other pilots. They'll take you out of here. We still have things to finish."

They nodded and disembarked as Kaiden took hold of the railing and looked at Chiyo. "Come on, Chi. We're heading out."

The infiltrator glanced at the officer at the console, who nodded and gave her a thumbs-up. She waved to her in thanks and scrambled aboard. The door shut as Wolfson turned the vessel toward the hangar's exit.

The ace made his way back to the cockpit. "So, how's he doing?"

"I don't know. It's a generic emergency signal and I can't make contact with him," Wolfson revealed. "He probably has his comms off for now, or at least has no long-range."

Kaiden stared at the screen that displayed a map of the academy and his eyes bulged at the number of hostiles either around the AC or headed toward it. "Good God. What the hell did he do?"

"Either they really want the place destroyed or they want something inside it. I would guess the latter since they don't seem to be firing at it. Many of them are simply standing outside the perimeter like they are trying to stop anyone from getting out or in." The head officer took his tablet out, placed it on the console, and pressed a few keys. "I'm ordering any nearby security bots to head that way. I'll need you to take over once we punch through and drop me on the roof."

"You're going in?" he asked and strapped himself in.

"That's my plan. I might get lucky and Sasha's already waiting for us, but those bots like to climb things and are annoyingly good at it too. He's probably hiding inside and I need to go in and get him."

"I should come down with you," he offered.

Wolfson waved him off. "You need to fly my ship. You're the only one besides Sasha I trust with it. Besides, who do you think will distract the bots outside?"

Kaiden nodded although he folded his arms as he thought it over. "Does that make me support or bait?"

"Two times out of three, support is merely a nice way to say bait." The giant chuckled but sobered when he caught sight of one of the cannons outside the window. "Hey, I have an idea. Get Chiyo in here."

The Arbiter bots advanced resolutely on the building. They had their directives—retrieve the codex and Master EI, eliminate all targets, and attempt to subdue potential recruits, but the items took priority. But as the first group of droids reached the door, they were engulfed in a bright flash and several of them were obliterated, with several more blown back in various conditions of damage.

The many other droids behind or around them focused on another orb that careened toward them to blast yet another group of them. Several linked together to create a stronger shield to protect the regiment, although they paid no attention to what was happening behind them. A sensor warned of a new arrival seconds before they were shot to dust by explosive rounds. Wolfson's ship flew overhead while cannon seven, clear across the island but with a clean line of sight to the outside of the Animus center, continued to fire as soon as a new shot was charged.

Kaiden pulled the ship up to the roof and fired at any bots that climbed the side of the building. Chief worked the shield and maximized the front while the vessel drifted around the ring of the roof to clear the path as the back walkway dropped. Wolfson emerged with his shotgun in hand. He leapt down, landed on a droid, and aimed to his right and fired at another. He charged to the door and bulldozed it off its hinges to gain access to the center.

It was time to save his new boss.

CHAPTER THIRTY-EIGHT

Wolfson kicked down the door to one of the halls and immediately, a duo of bots lunged at him, close enough that he was able to eliminate both with one shot. He proceeded down the stairs and activated a light on his shoulder pad, only for a sniper shot from below to shoot it off. The sniper vanished into the nearby room as he leapt down the remaining flights, brandishing his ax as he pounded into the carcass of an Arbiter droid.

He looked up as one of the improved models aimed a cannon at him with a group close behind it. Reflexively, he threw his ax and caught the side of the cannon which erupted and scattered the droids around it. Directly ahead, the sniper took aim across the way, but the head officer rolled out of the sightline and yanked out his hand cannon. He had fired several shots before the sniper activated a cloak. "Sasha, where are you, dammit?" he called. "I'll lose a kill because I'm busy worrying about you."

"You won't." A calm reply crackled over the comms and

a door at the other end of the building began to slide open. Wolfson caught the sniper reactivating their cloak. "Sasha!"

A figure appeared in the doorway and there was a loud crack followed by another thump. Sasha flipped his rifle and aimed it down as the head officer hurried over. The sniper's cloak fell away as quickly as it had activated.

"Humph," the giant grunted and slung his shotgun over his shoulder. "Were you simply waiting to make a grand entrance?"

"I was a few floors down, Wolfson," the commander explained as he stepped past his friend. "Dealing with some soldiers. One of them had a jamming device so I had to eliminate them first."

"It's good to see you, Officer Wolfson," Akello said as she stepped through the doorway behind the commander.

He smirked and adjusted his shotgun sling. "Aye, Akello, it's good to see you. It's also nice to see the chancellor hasn't forgotten his manners while taking you on a walk through this enemy-infested building."

Sasha looked at the other side of the room and hastily took aim at something and fired. Sparks and smoke burst and flurried in the corner of the room. "Crawler drone," he explained and turned as a small, spider-like droid fell from the ceiling "We should be on the move. The droids are only a couple of floors below us now."

Wolfson looked at the sniper "Should we take her for interrogation?" he asked.

The other man nodded, although he was obviously reluctant. "We don't have many options now. Laurie hasn't contacted me to let me know if he found anything so we need some way to get information."

"I agree with ya there." He heaved the unconscious sniper up and slung her over his shoulder. "All right, let's get moving before Kaiden gets bored and starts getting funny ideas."

"Do you think I should get my boots on the ground?" Kaiden yelled into the cabin.

"Are you an idiot?" Silas asked.

"That's…a stupid…question," Raul mumbled.

"Oh, hey, Raul is coming to," the enforcer noted.

Mack stretched. "I can't say I don't understand. We have real weapons now and they're simply sitting there."

"Not to mention that I'd rather die fighting than because Kaiden can't fly," Luke muttered as the ace made another sudden turn to fire on the bots below.

"Do you wanna give this a shot?" he retorted. "Chief, are you still tracking?"

"Yeah. It looks like they are coming up. Get ready to swing by." His eye narrowed as he changed to an annoyed red. *"I've tried to hack into the droids and mechs ever since we destroyed the disruptor, but nothing doing."*

"I have had similar issues as well, my friend." Kaitō agreed and appeared next to Chief on the screen.

The EI eyed the new arrival with a wide eye. *"Whoa, where the hell did you come from?"*

"Hey, Kaiden!" Wolfson's voice boomed out of the pilot's console. "We're coming up. Get your ass over here."

"Someone's cranky," he muttered.

"What was that?"

"I'm on my way, Wolfson," he responded and banked toward the Animus Center. As he did so, he took another look at the destruction of the campus and both his dorm and the cafeteria, in particular. The dorm was on fire and the cafeteria was in a shambles, at least half of it crushed under its own metal, glass, and stone.

He tensed but forced himself to put his focus on recovering his mentors. They would be needed in the fight to come.

In fact, they would all need each other for there to be victory after this.

CHAPTER THIRTY-NINE

*W*hen will the siege be done?
  Very soon.
Can't give me an ETA?

I would say in about an hour or less. Depends on the charge of the core.

That doesn't give me much time but I'll make do. You might want to hurry up and take your leave as well.

Dario put the tablet away and wondered what Damyen was up to. It didn't particularly bother him, but if he messed up badly, he would probably have a new assassination directive in short order.

He boarded his ship and glanced back as he walked up the rear bridge. Although it seemed such a waste, he had to agree with Merrick. It would be better to create a new symbol than to simply reuse an old one. And for that to happen, they would need to be rid of the old symbol.

That and they probably didn't have the forces to really take over the World Council. He would have loved to try. But as he looked at his tablet and saw that the remaining droids were being destroyed at a rather brisk rate, he acknowledged that now would be the best time to make his exit.

The bridge withdrew behind him and the door closed. He activated his ship's cloaking device—although he knew it wouldn't be enough to escape completely unnoticed. He was almost certain that the turrets guarding the outer ring of the city would fire upon any ship trying to leave at this point.

Or, at least, that would have been a problem if it wasn't for the encoder he took from the lab. It was rather annoying that it was the only one he could find, but one small headache saved a much bigger one. He sat in the pilot's seat and placed the chip into a slot on his console, smiling as the system booted up. It unfortunately did not give him full access to all systems on the cloud city or anything like that, but it would mean that the defenses wouldn't register him as suspicious and he could leave without problems.

But he wouldn't depart quite yet, merely find a suitable location to watch the fall of a symbol.

"Along with the attack on Nexus academy, there were simultaneous attacks all over the world. These were led by various terrorist organizations as well as black market mercenary companies seemingly under the employ of these terrorists. There have been no demands listed or even any explanation as to why these different organizations are even working with one another as many have conflicting interests."

The reporter continued to speak while Julio attempted to contact Kaiden, Sasha, or anyone associated with Nexus to try to find out what was happening—if they were even alive.

"Better news comes from Terra, as we have been assured by various high-ranking officers that the attempted takeover is almost at an end. We are told that the military will scour the entire city to be sure that no threats remain from these mysterious assailants and that the police have already started initial sweeps. They should soon have suspects in custody who can shed more light on the systematic attacks."

Laurie's shuttle finally found a landing zone. It appeared that they were the third shuttle to arrive, at least at this particular location. The doors opened and he, Cyra, and all the other technicians with them exited the vessel and studied the view of the city.

"It looks like they're mostly unharmed," Cyra said, her voice quiet as she frowned at the cityscape.

"I'm not sure we can exactly breathe a sigh of relief," the professor said, his tone a little short as he strode ahead. "With that colossus above us, we need to get as far away from here as possible. There is no point in surviving a slaughter only to be turned to glass by that monster's cannon."

"Where should we go?" she questioned and tried to keep pace with him.

"Seattle would be the obvious and easy option," he stated as his gaze darted around to check on Academy evacuees and seemingly looking for someone amongst the police and medical professionals. "Seattle has enough defenses to at least make the ship unlikely to simply barrel into it. Hell, if I can convince the mayor to give me access to the bio-sphere, I can convert it into a shield with enough tinkering."

"So we need to evacuate the entire town as well?" Cyra asked, her expression a little daunted. "Do we even have enough shuttles to do that?"

"That's what I'm trying to determine right now," he replied and tapped the shoulder of an officer assisting a newly landed shuttle. "Pardon me. Who is in charge here?"

The man shook his head. "Honestly, I couldn't really tell you. Most of the real leadership is on the front lines making sure those bots don't get into the city itself."

"I see. Whatever the case may be, I need to at least discuss evacuating the populace." Laurie pointed at the enormous vessel. "I'm sure you know that we are not truly safe while we are near that thing."

"It doesn't take a genius to understand that," the officer agreed. "We've notified nearby cities and are bringing together all the carriers and shuttles we can and have already warned the city to evacuate through the network."

"Did you decide on a destination?"

"We recommended Seattle as the closest available city for defensive reasons. But I can't imagine that many will want to risk still being within such a close range of that thing."

"Particularly if they are able to get Aurora online," the professor muttered and looked away for a moment before he returned his gaze to the officer. "Have you been able to make contact with the WC? I would imagine that even if they are in the middle of an important discussion or their usual prattle, this would get their attention."

The man's eyes widened for a moment before he drew in a sharp intake of breath and shook his head. "Right. Obviously, you wouldn't know. None of you would."

Laurie raised an eyebrow as Cyra stepped forward. "Know what?"

"The World Council building has been under attack, probably even before the Academy was," he explained. "The last I heard, they were still fighting to take it back."

His face paled alarmingly quickly. "The world council under attack?" he asked, his voice shaken. "By who? How did they get in?"

"You would think it would take an army, but from what I heard in the news, a small force was able to slip in and simply take it over from the middle section, lock the top floors, and push the personnel and guards down," the officer explained and looked briefly at the Academy. "They said they were fighting advanced bots, white and humanoid-looking like the ones that attacked the city and Nexus."

The professor pursed his lips. His color returned but it was an infuriated red. "This was what they prepared for? What was the purpose? Why spread their forces?" he muttered to himself. He returned his attention to the officer. "Did anything else happen? Was anyone else attacked?"

"Many people, unfortunately," the man replied with a nod. "Terrorist cells, gangs, all those bastards have blown things up since this began. I guess they used the chaos to their advantage and simply started all kinds of shit. In Sydney, Beijing, Vancouver, London, you name it. Most of the major cities have had to deal with it since the attack started."

Laurie nodded but remained silent as he moved passed the guard. Cyra nodded to the man in thanks and caught up to the professor, who stared at the colossus. "I should have focused on them more—exposed them—but I was too arrogant. I thought I had more time…" He covered his face with his hand and closed his eyes. "I have failed." She placed a hand on his shoulder to comfort him but suddenly, he stood tall, removed his hand from his face, and balled it into a fist. "But we will prevail! We will not let the Arbiters have their way."

Cyra stepped back, surprised by his outburst, but his declaration emboldened her. She looked at the enormous vessel and for the first time since it had appeared, she wasn't frightened by it. The massive craft wasn't a terror anymore. Instead, it was something to destroy.

CHAPTER FORTY

"Sir, the destroyers *Rammstein* and *Krokus* have arrived to join the blockade. I am attempting to contact them so we can link up for orders."

The captain shrugged where he leaned against the railing of the command deck as he looked out of the front window. "Yet more ships with nothing to do. We've held this blockade all day!" He grunted, his impatience clear in his voice. "We have enough ships here to obliterate half of Europe. Rather than wait here and twiddle our thumbs, we should put an end to this charade of an 'invasion' and assist in putting down the terrorist attacks over the world."

"It's a delicate situation, sir," the executive officer reminded him. "If this invader will not back down, they will be moved to desperate actions. You have to think of the collateral damage and loss of life if we simply try to destroy them. What about any council member still trapped in the building?"

"Elections will happen soon then, won't they?" the captain retorted and immediately straightened and held a hand up to calm the officer. "I joke, promise. I know that the troops in the building are making their way up. In fact, ensign, what is their progress?"

"According to the latest report, they are only four floors from their destination, sir."

He nodded and allowed himself a small grin. "Terrific. We might as well tell other ships to head out and do some real work."

"Sir, I've established a connection to *Rammstein* and *Krokus*, but they aren't responding."

The captain and officer looked at the speaker. "Did something go wrong with the comms on their way here?" the officer asked.

"Scan the ships for signs of damage and maybe try to send messages via the terminal," the captain ordered. Before the ensign could comply, his terminal deactivated, along with most of those on the command deck. "What the hell is—"

"Greetings, crew of the *Veles*," a deep but jovial voice said over the speakers. "My pardon for the sudden takeover, but my teams aboard the other ships had some complications and ended up on a course over to the front-line. I decided that since we were here, we should try out a new program of ours."

"They are trying to commandeer our systems," the captain snapped. "Purge them now."

"I think we'll only be able to take you and maybe two more at best," Damyen told him. "That should be fine, however, and more than I anticipated for today. It's been quite a stressful situation, I assure you, so it's nice that we can have one beneficial thing happen for once."

"Whoever you are, relinquish this ship," the captain ordered.

"You should prepare to do that yourself, Captain. I won't provide an alternative once we take you back to base," the chancellor warned. "Besides, you should thank us. Unlike all the other ships here, your crew, at least, will live."

Sweat trickled down the captain's brow. This was surely a simple intimidation tactic, right? There were now over sixty vessels present. They had no weapon capable of decimating an armada of this size and would need a device capable of tremendous power and destruction that could obliterate all or most of them in one strike. Did they have a nuke? A rapture cannon? This had to be a bluff. If these terrorists weren't affiliated with any larger corporation or government, they wouldn't have been able to create something—

As his mind frantically considered the implications, he caught another glimpse of Terra below and the answer occurred to him out of the blue—not create but destroy. He paled and looked around hastily as he hurried to his chair. "Get in contact with someone—anyone!" he ordered and tried to access his terminal. "Tell them to pull away!"

"It's too late now, dear Captain." Damyen chuckled. "We should find a safe distance."

As Izzy walked the field, attending to those who had made it through the tunnels and been escorted to the medical staff, a few shuttles came in and settled gently at a safe distance. She searched for her friends, anxious to see who else had made it.

So far, she had yet to find any of them, and the number of those who had made their way there thus far was frighteningly few.

When she walked past one of the makeshift medical tents, she noticed someone with their hair undone and whose clothes were distressed but recognized the doctor who examined one of the initiates.

"Doctor Soni," she cried and rushed inside.

The woman looked at her and exhaled a sigh of relief as she stood quickly and accepted her embrace. "It's good to see you, Isadora," she said, addressing the scout by her full name.

"Where's Amber? She made it with you, right?"

Soni pursed her lips and nodded. "She's all right, but…" The doctor drifted off for a moment and Izzy's concern mounted. "During our escape, we were pursued by soldiers as we made our way down the emergency hatch and, to cover our escape, Flynn and Marlo—"

She didn't need to finish. The scout's eyes widened in understanding and shock. "Where is she?"

Izzy walked into the bunker as others approached the doctor. The woman told her that Amber hadn't moved since they arrived and had said she simply needed time to compose herself. She had been down there for more than three hours now.

Quickly, she walked into the mostly barren gathering

area and in the corner, huddled into herself, was her friend. She crossed hastily to her, knelt, and placed a hand on her arm. "Amber?"

The battle medic looked up for a moment. Her eyes were sunken and her jaw clenched, but a spark of life flared in her when she recognized the scout. "Izzy?" she asked, her voice quiet.

She nodded and slid an arm around her to hold her as Amber did the same. "Your mom told me what happened with Flynn and Marlo," she whispered gently.

Amber nodded and drew small, sharp breaths. "They stayed behind so we could get away. I didn't see what happened—the door shut. I only heard...heard shots and something hitting the ground."

Izzy remained silent. Hearing it that way with no details and only the sounds to go on, a dark feeling threatened to come over her as the image came together.

"Could they have been taken?" her friend asked, as much to herself as to Izzy. "Many of the students... It's horrible to see it as the better option, but if they were taken, we can get them back, right?"

Izzy leaned in and gave her friend another hug. "Of course we can, and we will," she promised. "If they are there, we will get them back with all the others. Everyone lost something today, but I'm sure we will all do our best to get it back."

Amber nodded and held her tightly. "Thank you, Izzy." She uttered a soft sob but pulled away after a moment. Her eyes still contained sadness, but it was eclipsed by a new determination. "We need to go up top. I doubt we're in the clear simply because we made it across the bay."

She smiled. "I think most people are coming to that conclusion." She helped the medic up and they both headed to the exit of the bunker. "I think I heard some of the officers saying they ordered an evacuation of the town. That they would take the survivors to Seattle."

"We'll be close by, then," Amber muttered and her eyes narrowed in thought. "I hope we have the chance to destroy them before anyone else."

The girls shared a determined look as they ascended the stairs. "We won't let them have the satisfaction of keeping us on the run. Before long, we'll be back for what's ours."

The battle medic balled her fist. "Right." That was her only response as she walked out of the bunker and looked into the sky where the stars had barely begun to show themselves. She stared at the colossus. Flynn and Marlo were in there. She wanted to say she could feel it but she knew she was relying on hope.

Even so, she wouldn't let them take that from her.

CHAPTER FORTY-ONE

M errick watched each battle unfold. Dozens of screens displayed each conflict, all started under his direction. He felt each loss of life and would draw a sharp breath when he saw the fear in an Ark Academy student's eyes as they were captured. This was for the betterment of humanity but like any surgical improvement, the work was always visceral. The hope was that the outcome could mask it.

As he watched the fourth screen on which one of their Ark soldiers pushed down on a student from the Ark Ultra Academy in London, he received a message from Oliver Solos.

He and the other council members had reached the embassy, and he had already set to work listening in on what they planned to do in retaliation. He said that the fleets were mobilizing and would head down to Earth in a few short hours if the assault on the world council was not already put down. Merrick knew it would be finished by then, but they would probably still send the fleets once they saw how.

The embassy was its own issue, one that he and the others had debated for many days. They knew that every action would only stall defeat and they needed numbers and power to actually increase their chances to a point where victory was an option. He looked at the screen. Three out of five academies were now under their control and the other two would be shortly.

Damyen was still pirating ships. Combined with the total they had made in preparation, along with what he had now at the last report, they were looking at a fleet of sixty-three ships thus far. There might be a few more by the end of the week but it was hardly a force that would repel the embassy's forces. They also had general Nolan's flagship. The colossus was truly a marvel. Only one other had been created prior to the Arbiter Organization's and it had unfortunately been lost more than a decade before in a massive fight with the Omega Horde.

That thought reminded him that he needed to get in touch with Jiro to determine when they were supposed to arrive. They would need them soon to make up for the many other patsies lost in the various scuffles. He sent a message to Oliver and asked him to reach out to Jiro with his report and also to confirm that he had given the device to Nolan.

In only a minute, the man replied and stated that he would talk to Jiro and that he had delivered the device as well as a prototype to Damyen upon request, although he didn't have much of a clue of what it would be used for.

The AO leader looked at the map overview of Terra.

Several dots were pulling away from the blockade and he wondered how the Russian chancellor had managed to achieve that. He might have been a loose cannon at times, but he backed it with results, a trait to admire.

The embassy, he reminded himself. He needed to stay focused. So much was going on right now but once they sent their fleets, that could end this before they could really build traction. They had agreed that there were two ways to take the problem on and right now, it depended on the general and Lena to see which they would go with, either the pragmatic choice or the violent one.

"Get your asses on board. We're boosting out!" Kaiden yelled to Sasha, Akello, and Wolfson as they scrambled on board.

"We've already boosted her enough. Too much and you could melt the jets," the giant warned as he strode to the cockpit.

"Haven't you sprung for the reinforced inner lining?" the ace complained as he shut the rear dock and quickly whipped the vessel around to avoid a charged shot by one of the mechs below.

The head officer flattened a hand against the wall to steady himself. "Dammit, boyo, give me the controls."

"It's good to have you onboard, Commander," Jaxon said and helped Sasha to the bench.

Chiyo came up and hugged Akello. "I'm glad to see you safe."

"I'm glad to be safe," the head monitor admitted and slid

one arm around her while the other held the EI drive. "It's kinda full circle that you guys would be the ones to come and rescue me."

"Have any of you heard from Laurie since the ship shut down?" Sasha asked, interrupting them.

The infiltrator pulled back and shook her head. "Even when we destroyed the disruptor device, it took time for us to re-establish a connection to the network. And it's been so hectic that we haven't been able to contact anyone."

"There should have been enough time for the Academy network to be back in working order—unless they have destroyed the servers in the tech department," Akello said.

Sasha nodded and retrieved his oculars. "I can check the map—"

"Sasha!" Kaiden cried and startled all the passengers. "Can you talk some sense into Wolfson? He's trying to get me to drop him off at the security station."

"I still have men and women on Academy grounds," the head officer yelled in response. "I can't leave them here."

The commander nodded to Akello, stood, and headed to the cockpit where the large man attempted to haul Kaiden out of the pilot's chair. "Idiot," he said brusquely. "I still need to get us to a safe distance—which, if you haven't noticed, is a hell of a long distance away. Besides, you were the one who tried to convince me that retreat was for the best."

"Yes, for you," his friend retorted. "You should get out of here. You've done more than can be asked right now, but I have a job to—"

"And I don't, Wolfson?" Sasha asked. The head officer's

grasp slackened for a brief moment and Kaiden pulled himself away and changed course to fly toward the mountains. "I don't like it either, but we need to be prepared for the counteroffensive once we are able to reconvene and get assistance from the military."

"It's...different between me and you Sasha," Wolfson argued. "You're the chancellor now and need to be with the students and get them to safety. I can't simply leave—"

"Issue orders for a full retreat," the commander said. "If there are more shuttles available, tell your guards to sweep the island and find any remaining students or staff they can. Then, they can activate their personal beacons and be picked up. That would be more of a help than merely fighting the droids."

The large man sighed and finally nodded. "Fine. You're right, but I won't sit around for months while the WC gets their shit together. We'll retaliate soon, right?"

Sasha was silent. He wanted to but realistically, he couldn't give him an answer yet. Kaiden finally set a course toward the town and they stared with grim expressions as more pods ascended toward the ship in the distance. He briefly contemplated shooting them down—that would have to be more of a mercy than letting the enemy have them, right?

He shook it out of his mind. No, they would get them back. He had to rely on what everyone said, that there was a reason they had taken them and that they could get them back. His lip flared with a sharp pain on his lip and he realized he'd bit it too hard in his frustration. The three soldiers in the cockpit looked equally disgruntled. All of them were used to running operations and completing their missions or, at the very least, making sure the enemy had hell to pay.

They were all going against their instincts on this one, having to rely on tactics and on hope rather than action or strategy. Kaiden simply turned away from the pods and focused on the horizon.

"General, there is an incoming call from the leader."

Nolan nodded. "Put it onscreen."

A holoscreen appeared to the side of his chair. Merrick's face appeared in the display and his bemused grin caught the general off guard. He couldn't tell what the leader was thinking—was he pleased?

"General," Merrick said.

"Sir," he replied.

"Well done so far, but I must press you a little—or perhaps I should say Lena. The world council will be dealt with soon enough, but we need to deal with the issue of the embassy. That depends on you."

"Right, sir." He nodded and reached to the side of the screen. "I'll get Lena on the line."

It took several rings but the tech finally answered. Her artificial eye dimmed as she appeared on a separate screen. "I'm about ready— Sir!" She yelped in surprise as she registered that Merrick was also on the call.

"Evening, Lena," he said smoothly. "I wanted to check your progress. The general was kind enough to get you the EI. Is it ready yet?"

She nodded hastily. "Yes, sir. I've actually finally put

everything in place and was about to finish the reconstruction."

"Ah, fortunate timing then," he responded. "Oliver has told me that he's heard whispers of the embassy preparing their response, and quite soon, I believe. I'm sure you'd rather take time to test your new toy, Lena, but we'll need it sooner rather than later."

"Of course, sir," she said and glanced at Nolan. "Do you still have the device?"

He nodded and produced the round drive from his chest pocket. "I'll have one of my technicians install it at once."

Merrick's smile became a little more apparent and widened slowly. "Very good. That should give the EI access to the embassy's systems once it is within range."

The general looked at the Nexus map. "We're only mopping up at this point, sir. I don't believe leaving will swing this in their favor. Would you like me to depart immediately?"

"Do you have the students?"

He looked at the current total. "Approximately fifty-two percent of the student body has been captured, but only forty-three percent are on board. I can return after this task is complete."

"See that you do, General. You shouldn't leave your troops behind," the leader said, his tone almost playful. "And there are still secrets that need to be unearthed. Speaking of which, when you have the opportunity, instruct the EI to locate a file on the embassy marked AS_000. We'll need that for our future army."

"Of course, sir. I assume it's connected to the Animus?" Nolan enquired.

Merrick looked away, lost briefly in a memory. He ran a hand through his hair and shook his head. "It's older than the Animus project," he revealed. "It would have been the future of humanity—a future I played a part in and one I died for."

CHAPTER FORTY-TWO

"Everyone, get to a ship!" Haldt ordered as he and Eckles raced into the hangar. The pilots they had escorted had already dashed toward the remaining craft. "There is no time to dawdle."

"No kidding. I'm down to the last two cannons." The officer at the console sighed when one of the screens went black. "Shit, make that last one."

"To every member of the security team," a deep, accented voice said in the officer's comms.

"It's Wolfson!" Eckles stated. "Is he broadcasting to everyone?"

"It sounds like it. Listen up," Haldt ordered.

"I'm issuing a full retreat order with immediate effect," the head officer said, frustration evident in his voice. "You are still to do your job while you make your way out of the base, however. Help anyone you can on your way out. Group together and stay safe. We'll need you to take our island back."

"Retreat?" Eckles sounded indignant. "I know it's the

obvious choice right now, but it's strange to hear it come from Wolfson."

"Ever since the first volley of bots, this has been merely a game of time." Haldt sighed, tapped the shoulder of the officer at the console, and pointed to one of the ships. She nodded and made her way to it after she set the final cannon to auto. "You can tell he obviously wasn't pleased about it."

"No kidding." The other man sighed and stepped beside the security captain. "We still have our part to play so let's rescue whoever else we can. The ship above hasn't made a move yet and let's hope it stays that way for a while longer."

His companion nodded, but as he turned to look at the console for one last look at the grounds before he boarded his shuttle, he noticed that the sky had begun to brighten and the twilight became clearer. It took a moment before he realized that the reason was because the ship had begun to move from above the island.

He sucked in a surprised breath. "What the hell?"

"What the hell is it doing?" Sasha asked and peered out of the window to watch as the colossus began to fly away from the island. Not only fly away, he realized. In fact, it ascended to break above the clouds.

"I don't feel very triumphant," Cameron with a disgruntled look at the others. "Is it getting help?"

"Do you think it needs help right now?" Luke asked. "Good God, I hope not."

"It looks like the thrusters are about to activate and go full force," Chiyo pointed out. "Is it heading into space?"

"Sasha? Sasha?" a frantic voice called out over the comm.

"Laurie?" the commander answered. "I'm here. What's wrong?"

"Oh, thank goodness. I've tried to reach you ever since we made it off the island."

"I've had to keep my comms off until recently," he explained. "You're seeing the colossus leave, correct?"

"It's hard to miss," the professor stated dryly. "But I don't know where it could be headed. They should still be hobbled by my hacking attempt. They've either resorted to controlling everything manually, had a spare EI installed and cleaned up the systems...or..."

"Or what, Laurie?"

His friend uttered a pained gasp. "I'm so sorry, Aurora."

* * *

As the colossus breached the clouds, Nolan took his seat. "Make sure the shields are focused on the front. I expect instant retaliation until we can get into range," he ordered and took a moment to look at their new EI. Currently, it simply displayed an image of its head, which glowed a bright blue that occasionally shifted to white and dark, cloudy eyes. "Have the cannon primed as well. Should you fail, I doubt we can sufficiently destroy the station, but we should be able to cause massive damage before making our retreat."

"Understood, General." The EI nodded. "However, I shall not lose."

He smiled, crossed his legs, and leaned back. "I'm glad to hear it, Aurora. Connect to the embassy's systems as soon as we're in range." She nodded and the avatar disappeared as Lena walked up to the side of Nolan's chair. "Magnificent work, Lena, and well-timed too," he said cheerfully. "What made you keep its name?"

The hacker shrugged. "I thought it sounded pretty."

Nolan raised an eyebrow but shrugged as one of the crewmen shouted. "Brace for boost. Activating internal gravity field."

The internal gravity field should negate the sudden shift from the ship's boost but Nolan still made sure to sit up straight and press himself against his chair. Lena walked to the bridge and found a spare seat as a countdown began. A blaring alarm sounded when it reached the last five seconds and when it hit zero. The view outside the ship became a blur as their speed increased massively. They broke into the stratosphere, then the mesosphere in quick succession. When they neared the line of the thermosphere, they began to slow until they approached the exosphere. From there, the colossus gradually resumed its normal speed and Nolan could see their target.

In the distance was the massive, cross-shaped station that housed the current galactic alliance. It was several times the size of even his ship and was well-armed as well —and apparently, had numerous ships docked there as well. Now, many of them scrambled to meet the new arrival.

"We're getting hailed, sir," a crewman announced.

"Hold it for a moment, if you would," Nolan stated and displayed a little more cockiness than he had thus far. "Bring us in closer. Is the cannon ready?"

"It is, sir," the crewman confirmed, his tone tinged with shock. "It should have taken longer but the EI had it ready in only two minutes."

"She's already proving a good investment." He chuckled.

"We're still getting hailed sir, and the ships are mobilizing and locking in on our position."

The general looked at Lena, who nodded and studied the graph on the screen. "Only a few more seconds," he said

"They're firing!" He looked up as dozens of lights streaked in his direction.

"Expanding shields, concentrating at the front of the ship," Aurora's monotone voice responded. As soon as the lasers impacted, ripples of light covered the colossus as the shields defended against the attacks.

"The shields won't last under this assault, sir! We only have—"

"In position. Assuming control of embassy systems." The blasts continued to batter the colossus, but Nolan had already felt relief as soon as Aurora spoke. *"I will now retaliate."*

He smiled and gestured with a casual wave of his hand. "Please do."

The embassy's cannons that had previously been trained on the vessel now turned to aim at all the ships below. They fired with frightening precision and all shots struck dead-on at weak points in the various ships. The general watched them break apart as if they had been struck by a spear from the heavens. Considering the power behind those cannons, it wasn't a farfetched idea at all.

Nolan leaned back and his grin broadened as some of the ships broke away and tried to retreat. "We might not have many pieces in this game, but we have the right ones, it seems." He chuckled and glanced at Lena, who nodded.

"Do we still have the embassy's hail, by chance?" he asked.

"We do, sir."

"Go ahead a put it on now." He was greeted by two stony faces as several embassy crew members raced around frantically behind them. "Greetings, gentleman. You wanted to talk?" he said glibly and caught their attention.

One of the men narrowed his eyes, both in fury and in confusion. "Wait—I know you. I've seen you somewhere before."

"Really, now? Funny, I thought all mention of me would have been scrubbed," he muttered and shook his head. "It doesn't matter. I'm sure you've realized that the embassy is no longer under your control."

"Are you a damn fool?" one of them yelled. "You attack the embassy? What have you accomplished? There are terrorist attacks taking place as we speak and thousands of people are dying!"

"I can assure you that we have no intention to needlessly kill those we will need for the fight," he promised, but this only caused confusion among the two. "We shall board soon but won't stay long. I merely need to make sure the station is ready for our leader."

"Do you think we'll simply let you on here?" one of them asked, a trace of laughter in his tone. "There are battalions from all races here. The Sauren alone will—"

"Ah, yes, speaking of friends—how close are our friends, Aurora?" Nolan asked the EI nonchalantly.

"They are approaching the exit gate now and will arrive in only a few moments."

"Wonderful. Please be sure to deactivate the gates once they've arrived." She nodded and vanished once more as he stood and approached the monitor. "The embassy is merely one of the accomplishments the four races of the galaxy have accomplished together and a small one at that." He stretched his arms wide. "Think of what we can accomplish from here. I remember the opening ceremony, although I was only a teenager when it happened." He lowered his arms and linked his hands behind his back. "I do not fear the other races, although I do expect you to put up a fight." Nolan gestured behind the two men, where a turret dropped from the ceiling and aimed at them. "I can tell you it will be a closer fight than you believe."

"W-who do you want to s-speak to?" one of them stammered.

"As far as I am concerned, none of you are truly the leaders here," he retorted and with a snap of his fingers, the turret shot the two men—as well as the console, apparently, as the screen went black. "He'll arrive shortly."

"Incoming in gates three, five, eight, nine, and ten," Aurora announced. Dozens of dark ships appeared in flashes of light behind the embassy and a smile crossed his lips.

"The Omega Horde has arrived."

CHAPTER FORTY-THREE

"Are you sure you don't want to join me?" Dario asked on the screen while Merrick finished getting dressed. "Admittedly, there isn't exactly much time left but you could use the transporter—"

"Nolan has the embassy in his grasp and the Horde has also arrived," the leader responded dismissively. "I have to address my future subjects."

The assassin chuckled. "You certainly seem to be in a mood now, don't you?"

He paid him no mind and focused on the task at hand. "When you are done, meet me at the embassy. From there, we will decide on the future of the mission."

"And I get to be a part of it?" he asked. "I have something of a one-track mind, you know."

Merrick buttoned his coat and glanced at the screen. "Do you think about the future much, Dario?"

"A little now and then, not much more."

The leader didn't respond right away and instead, studied his reflection in the mirror. "I would recommend you spend more time doing that. After all, with this, we are one step closer to actually having a future to look forward to."

Wolfson had taken over the pilot's seat and hoped to use the time while the colossus was gone to rescue more students. Kaiden was one of the first out of the dropship. He helped his friends out of the craft but the security team decided to stay with the head officer when he returned.

"Kaiden!" a familiar voice called. He looked around and located Laurie and Cyra, who hurried toward them.

He raised an arm to wave at them when someone ran past him. Chiyo raced over to Cyra and hugged her tightly in relief. "I'm glad you're safe."

"I'm glad you're safe too," Cyra replied and gestured at Laurie. "It was actually because of the professor that we got out at all."

"A small victory." He sighed. "Compared to my tragic mistake."

"If that's what you want to call it," she retorted. "You haven't really explained what happened with the ship."

"Indeed, Laurie," Sasha said when he appeared behind the group as Wolfson took off. "You said something about Aurora? What happened, exactly?"

"She was taken, Sasha," the professor explained. "When we tried to take control of the ship's EI, she offered to work the device to increase the success rate and we played right into their hands. They lost their EI but they stole Aurora."

The commander looked at the sky, where the colossus had once been. "At the cost of sounding dispassionate, I don't see the issue. Aurora was your personal EI, which means she's tethered to you and your devices. Beyond that, I doubt they have a system that could effectively handle her."

"They apparently do," his friend muttered and folded his arms as he looked down. "If not, Aurora should have been able to break away easily and return to me. I wasn't able to get her back. After a confrontation with their general, I had little choice but to escape at the time—"

"Their general? You saw him?" the commander asked. Kaiden and his friends gathered around.

"Only briefly. He mostly mocked me the entire time and said his name was General Nolan."

"Nolan?" Sasha looked suddenly thoughtful and placed a finger against his commlink. "That sounds familiar. Let me ask Wolfson if he—"

"Brace! We're heading up!" the head officer shouted.

"Wolfson, what's the matter?" Sasha yelled over the roar of the dropship's engines over the link.

"The damn barrier went back up. Everyone is trapped inside."

"The barrier?" Sasha and Laurie looked across the bay at a translucent white dome that had formed around the island.

Chief appeared in Kaiden's HUD *"Kaiden, I have a call from Julio."*

"Julio? Nothing's happening in Seattle, I hope." He stepped away from the group. "Connect us, Chief."

"Kaiden? Are you there, Kaiden?" the man asked and his voice sounded stressed and shaky.

"I'm here, Julio."

"Oh, thank God. Man, shit's been crazy since that colossus showed up at the island. There have been terrorist attacks all over the world, the WC building is under attack—"

"The council? By who?" His startled question caught Chiyo and Genos' attention.

"The same guys who attacked you—or the same droids, at least," Julio explained. "It looks like the worst is over, though. The last report said they were close to getting into the central chamber where the head honcho was located. A few of the ships are even starting to pull away to go and hel…at oth…"

"Julio? Hey, Julio?!" Kaiden poked his commlink like that would reconnect the call any faster. "Chief, can you clean it up?"

"Something is overriding the connection and switching the call."

"My tablet is rumbling," Genos stated. He retrieved the device and the three friends huddled around it. On the screen was the view of a large cloud city with a multitude of ships surrounding it.

"Terra, the home of the world council," Chiyo noted.

"Chief, who's sending this?" the ace asked as he noticed other students and officers taking their devices out, apparently all seeing the same thing.

"I can't say. It looks like the connection keeps hopping around. The better question is why?"

There wasn't anything noticeable in the air, no change in scent or smell or anything like that. Perhaps the citizens in Terra would have noticed a small increase in temperature and the ground a little hotter in certain places. But most of them would probably simply chalk that up to the fear and anxiety caused by the attack on the WC building. They didn't have anything to worry about, right? After all, they had been assured by the military that they would have everything restored soon and that they would be protected.

One of the power stations turned off briefly, followed by a second. They both came back on but only for a short while before all four turned off. Confusion was the immediate result. A few people turned to the military personnel for answers, although only a handful of them had any idea —the several dozen workers who monitored the cloud city's power, it's central core.

For one of these men, it took only a couple of moments for everything to click into place. He did not have time to panic or to try to start an evacuation. Instead, he simply held his wife close as the four pillars reactivated at the same time and the ground began to crack and heat to its upper limits.

Then, as several ships in the back of the blockade suddenly activated their thrusters and rocketed away, the cloud city erupted. The WC building and its entire sector were the first to go, but the force of the explosion expanded rapidly to envelop the first few ships in the line. This was quickly followed by almost the entire left half of the station erupting to obliterate much of the blockade and send both sharp and flaming debris rocketing to the ocean below. The side of Terra still mostly intact began to plummet with nothing left to keep it fully airborne when its engines gave way. Thousands of lives had gone in a moment and thousands more were about to be lost when it plunged into the sea.

One of the modern achievements of man and a symbol of their unity and advancement as a species was destroyed in a single day.

Kaiden's eyes widened, Chiyo fell to her knees with her hands to her lips, and Genos almost dropped his tablet.

"I am…sorry," the Tsuna murmured, clearly feeling the need to say something even if he could not decide what.

The ace was speechless. He had never seen destruction on that level before, even in the Animus. It seemed the reality of everything he was familiar with had descended into the chaos of sheer annihilation.

"Good evening, people of Earth," a voice announced. He looked up and forced himself forward as Genos raised the tablet again. Onscreen, a man with slicked-back dark hair and piercing silver eyes that contrasted sharply with his tan skin stared ahead with only a dark wall behind him.

"How is he broadcasting this to everyone?" Kaiden asked aloud.

"I actually have a destination this time. It says this is coming from the embassy's emergency channel."

Genos and Kaiden looked at one another, wide-eyed. "The embassy?"

"I am Merrick Rayne, the leader of the Arbiter Organization," the man announced. The ace tensed as rage surged within him and he looked at Sasha and Laurie to see their reactions at finally seeing the leader announce himself. Instead of determination or anger, they both looked pale like they had seen a ghost.

"I am the one who has orchestrated all the attacks today with assistance and planning from my associates," he continued. "I'm sure you have many questions and when I am ready, I will answer them all. But know that as of right now, I have done away with the World Council and am currently in the process of taking control of the embassy."

"What the hell?" Kaiden murmured. Chiyo looked at him and he helped her up as Merrick continued.

"I know that the horrors today will make you hate me. But in time, that will subside."

It seemed crazy that he actually believed that. With the enormous and perhaps immeasurable number of people who had died that day, this could easily be the worst loss of life on the planet ever. Given the tragedy that they had witnessed, it was almost impossible to think of a goal that could justify all that had happened.

"There was no other way. Without a doubt, there is a horror beyond what I have done coming to our galaxy, and we need to be prepared." Merrick displayed six different maps, one of which Kaiden was able to recognize instantly. "Decades ago, we prepared a failsafe. Once the vastness of space became a new frontier for us, we had to be ready for whatever might lurk beyond. At least, that was the initial promise. That was soon forgotten in favor of complacency, but no longer." Each of the maps flipped to their sides to reveal a holographic image of several different buildings, including one of the Nexus central tower. "We created the Ark Academies and named them as such so they would be what harbored and saved us from the potential threats of the galaxy. They have been used as testing grounds when they should be proving grounds. I have the means to make them what they should have been, and humanity will be the saviors of not only our planet but of this system."

Everyone on the field looked at one another and many looked at Laurie and Sasha, both of whom grimaced with quiet fury at the man on screen.

"If you want a future for us, be ready. You will have the opportunity to save it," the man said and his gaze hardened as he continued. "If you struggle and fight against my forces, that will only end in your pain and our doom." He stood tall. "But if I must make you subservient, so be it. I will see to it that we live on."

The screen went dark when the connection was lost. The field was silent, some faces grim, others confused, and many grieving.

Kaiden looked at Sasha and Laurie and walked up to them. "You know who that guy is, right?"

The professor lowered his tablet as Sasha nodded. "We might."

"Might? I saw your faces when he appeared."

"If he is who we think he is, he's been dead for over a decade," Laurie explained.

The ace didn't budge. "He seems very alive right now."

He fixed his two mentors with a questioning look. "We won't listen to him, will we?"

The commander shook his head. "Of course not, but we should find out what it is—"

"Look at what he's done!" he exclaimed. "Even only to us! Add on top of that all the attacks, the destruction of Terra, and now, he's taking over the embassy? For what? Some vague threat that he probably saw while drugged out?"

"I don't think anyone would have the drive or ability to put together the resources and effort it would have taken to make this happen if they were merely an addict." Laurie sighed.

"I don't care what he believes. I'll die fighting that insane son of a bitch before I ever help him. He wants the Academy, right? We'll start by taking it back. From there, we can get the other academies out of his hands.."

"We would still need the might of the military," Sasha explained. "Even with all the destruction, most of the force must still remain."

"How long will it take for them to recover?" Laurie asked. "To quell the attacks, regroup, and secure the cities? And without the central command of the WC, things will be chaotic for some time."

"Then we'll have to do it ourselves until they get their shit together." This time, it wasn't Kaiden who spoke but Luke. "Look, I'm not saying we force everyone to take up arms or anything. But most of us here are soldiers, right? Everyone is trained to fight in some fashion. We were caught unprepared and overwhelmed, but we're still here. We can take it to them now."

"The more we delay and the more we hide, it simply gives the enemy time to gather more power," Jaxon added and stepped into the group. "Whatever advantages we have now will matter little over time."

"And they took our friends too!" Amber and Izzy broke away from the crowd. "They took all those students and Flynn and Marlo—"

"What?" Kaiden gasped, clenched his fist, and looked around at the evacuees. "I don't know who is a soldier here and whether you're a master or an initiate. Like Luke said, no one here is being forced—at least not by me—to help us take the Academy back. But you have to know that they will come for all of us eventually. That won't be a choice."

There were murmurs of agreement, whispers, and mutterings in the crowd. "This bastard says he's doing this for our future," he continued. "I was planning my future—hell, because of Nexus, I actually have a future I give a damn about. I don't know what his plans are for us are, but I didn't put all my blood, sweat, and tears into this for him to decide for me. They attacked us, killed our friends and mentors, kidnapped others, and he wants to act like he's a messiah? I say that if he wants humanity to save itself, that's what we'll do by stopping him."

"And I will be happy to aid you, my friend," Genos stated.

Jaxon nodded beside him. "I as well."

"And me!" another Tsuna in the crowd offered.

"So, are we doing this now?" Cameron chuckled and held his weapon up. "I was born for this."

"Same here!" Mack shouted, and more and more people joined in—students who wanted to take back their home and initiates who'd had their first taste of war wiped the tears from their faces clean and stood to shout their agreement. Police and security officers held their weapons up or saluted.

Kaiden smiled as the crowd became exuberant and any feeling of despair or hopelessness gave way to camaraderie and determination. Sasha walked up beside him. "To think I had once worried that I had given you the wrong advice," he said and placed a hand on his shoulder. "But you have become a fine ace."

He chuckled. "Thanks. I'm glad to see I'm not merely being bullheaded."

"In certain situations, that is what is needed." The commander looked at the island as the dome's light grew thicker and obscured it from view. "Come on, let us prepare. We will see it again."

"Do you think it will be soon?" he asked as they walked through the crowd.

"I think you're too impatient for it not to be," Sasha replied as the crowd began to make their way to the shuttles to prepare to reclaim what was theirs.

Kaiden and friends are now available in audio at Amazon, Audible and iTunes. Check out book one, INITIATE, performed by Scott Aiello.

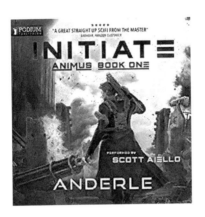

Check out book one at Amazon

(Book two - four are also available in audio, with more coming soon.)

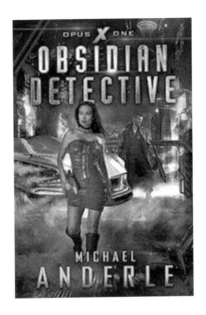

Available now at your favorite ebook stores.

Two Rebels whose Worlds Collide on a Planetary Level.

On the fringes of human space, a murder will light a fuse and send two different people colliding together.

She lives on Earth, where peace among the population is a given. He is on the fringe of society where authority is how much firepower you wield.

She is from the powerful, the elite. He is with the military.

Both want the truth – but is revealing the truth good for society?

Two years ago, a small moon in a far off system was set to be the location of the first intergalactic war between humans and an alien race.

It never happened. However, something was found many are willing to kill to keep a secret.

Now, they have killed the wrong people.

How many will need to die to keep the truth hidden?

As many as is needed.

He will have vengeance no matter the cost. *She will dig for the truth. No matter how risky the truth is to reveal.*

Available now from Amazon and other Digital Book Stores

AUTHOR NOTES - MICHAEL

DECEMBER 8, 2019

It was never about him... About Kaiden...

Yeah, yeah it was ;-)

We are in the middle of a massive battle for the future of humanity against aliens. The challenge is that those doing atrocious things are humans against other humans because they believe a certain path is the correct one.

And they are willing to kill a large number of innocent people now, on the chance it will save a large portion of humanity later.

This concept is so screwed up (and yet still believed today). I have challenges when considering the arguments for both sides.

For example: "We need to kill some today to prepare humanity for an awful tomorrow."

That's just a horrible argument.

1) These are innocents who would have gone on to produce more people for the future. If you are planning a war, wouldn't you want those people for armed support?

2) Assuming you are using golem-type fighters (thus reducing the need for fighters), you still need a large enough population that it doesn't get wiped out. Further, what are the chances you have just killed the Michelangelo of the future generation? Seriously, how many geniuses have we killed in the past who might have provided a different future for humanity?

3) Spilled blood does bad things to people. Not everyone can kill and be immune to the mental, emotional, and perhaps ethical quandaries that affect them in life. Future humanity is going to be affected for at least a couple of generations due to this horrible war.

4) What would someone say if the vision of the future doesn't occur? "Oops" just doesn't seem to cut it. "I had good intentions" doesn't either. With the sheer amount of effort that is being expended (and I do find this a viable if idiotic method of trying to protect humanity), one could surmise there should have been a second choice.

5) Well, actually, the more I think about #4, the more I realize it is the acquisition of resources (raw as well as manufacturing and income) that was the point. If you tried to start from scratch, getting to scale would be a huge challenge.

While humans live, we authors will never lack for antagonists.

THANK YOU

We are almost at the end of the series. Just two more books, and Kaiden's school career will be finished.

I doubt most readers saw this as his finale.

The sad thing is, I absolutely believe the horror we are witnessing in the stories can happen in the future. Just give humanity enough time.

Ad Aeternitatem,

Michael Anderle

BOOKS BY MICHAEL ANDERLE

For a complete list of books by Michael Anderle, please visit

www.lmbpn.com/ma-books/

All LMBPN Audiobooks are Available at Audible.com and
iTunes. For a complete list of audiobooks visit:

www.lmbpn.com/audible

CONNECT WITH THE AUTHORS

Michael Anderle Social
  Website:
  http://lmbpn.com

Email List:
  http://lmbpn.com/email/

Facebook Here:
  https://www.facebook.com/OriceranUniverse/
  https://www.
facebook.com/TheKurtherianGambitBooks/
  https://www.facebook.com/groups/
320172985053521/ (Protected by the Damned Facebook
Group)

Printed in Poland
by Amazon Fulfillment
Poland Sp. z o.o., Wrocław

55987000R00186